R.N.F. (RICHARD) SKINNER a writer by inclination, and a men for remuneration. He has publish (as Richard Skinner), and three works of ...... *Crazy...* (SilverWood 2020), a collection of short stories and comedy sketches, *After All...* (SilverWood 2022), and the novella *These Years: 1973* (SilverWood 2024), to which the current work is a sequel. He has also composed lyrics for a range of songs including the Christmas musical *Bethlehem!*

As well as being a member of the famous *Footlights* club while an undergraduate at Cambridge University, he also co-founded and performed extensively with the cabaret-revue team Seventh Sense. He continues to write and perform sketch-based comedy.

Though a Londoner by upbringing, he has lived in Exeter for many years. He is a qualified social worker, and in 2012 he was awarded a doctorate from Exeter University for his thesis on religion and evolutionary theory. He lives with his wife, three hens, a dog and a cat.

For further information about his books please visit his website at rnfskinner.com or contact him at richardskinner.exeter@gmail.com.

Also by R N F Skinner

Fiction
Still Crazy… (SilverWood 2020)
After All… (SilverWood 2022)
These Years: 1973 (SilverWood 2024)

Poetry (as Richard Skinner)
Leaping & Staggering (Dilettante 1988/1996)
In the Stillness: based on Julian of Norwich (Dilettante 1990/2013)
The Melting Woman (Blue Button 1993)
Still Staggering (Dilettante 1995)
Echoes of Eckhart (Cairns/Arthur James 1998)
The Logic of Whistling (Cairns 2002)
Invocations (Wild Goose 2005)
Colliding With God (Wild Goose 2016)
A brief poetry of time (Oversteps 2017)
The Colour of Water (Dilettante 2023)

THESE YEARS:
1986

R.N.F. SKINNER

SilverWood

Published in 2025 by SilverWood Books

SilverWood Books Ltd
14 Small Street, Bristol, BS1 1DE, United Kingdom
www.silverwoodbooks.co.uk

Copyright © R.N.F. Skinner 2025

The right of R.N.F. Skinner to be identified as the author of this
work has been asserted in accordance with the Copyright,
Designs and Patents Act 1988 Sections 77 and 78.

All rights reserved. No part of this publication may be reproduced,
stored in a retrieval system, or transmitted in any form or by any means,
electronic, mechanical, photocopying, recording or otherwise,
without prior permission of the copyright holder.

This is a work of fiction. Names, characters, places and incidents
either are products of the author's imagination or are used fictitiously.
Any resemblance to actual events or locales or persons,
living or dead, is entirely coincidental.

ISBN 978-1-80042-302-2 (paperback)
Also available as an ebook

British Library Cataloguing in Publication Data
A CIP catalogue record for this book is
available from the British Library

Page design and typesetting by SilverWood Books

For the "10 Selwyn Gardeners" and our partners

1986

i

It had been both exhausting and exhilarating. The artistic wealth of Italy was overwhelmingly wonderful and yet she had seen only a tiny fraction of it – but, oh, what a fraction! Florence being her last port of call, the Uffizi had blown her away – and yet, gloriously, she was actually a part of this wonderful world of art. Of Art. *She was a part of it!* She was accepted as being a legitimate authority. Well, trainee authority, strictly speaking. But in representing the gallery where she had been working since the previous spring, just over a year ago, she undoubtedly had some prestige.

*

Her meetings with the directors and staff of the various Italian galleries, in particular the discussions with the teams devoted to conservation and restoration, had taught her an immense amount. More, probably, than her entire university course. Though, of course, without her academic qualification in art history, she would never have been welcomed behind the scenes, or been asked to give an informal talk on American folk art, or been invited to contribute an article to a prestigious journal. At least, she assumed the journal was prestigious, though she hadn't heard of it before. In any case, she would have to get clearance from Gilly…

Ruth Whitehead, twenty-five, still full of Italy and its wonders, closed her eyes and leaned back in the plane seat while other passengers continued to board and fuss with overhead lockers. She felt a bit of a mess. Her hair, long and dark brown, definitely needed a wash – in fact, more than a wash, as the roots were beginning to show. And her clothes were rumpled. She refused to dwell on how ill-packed her suitcase and backpack were. When asked at the check-in, "Did you pack your bags yourself?", she had nearly replied, "Not pack so much as randomly stuff!" Anyway, who cares? Soon she would be in the air and on her way to England for a long weekend of rest and relaxation before heading home to Boston. Or would it be all that restful? Hard to say. Perhaps it had been over-ambitious to tack these coming few days in England on to the end of her Italian trip. However, once the idea had been seeded in her mind – the sower being Aunt Lou – she hadn't been able to forget it.

*

When Ruth's father, George, died the previous fall, Gilly Carter, director of the Boston Art Foundation & Gallery, had given her generous compassionate leave, allowing her to return for a while to where her mother still lived in north-west Massachusetts. She made all the necessary funeral arrangements and, with Lou, had contacted a whole range of her parents' friends and numerous relatives, her mother being too prostrated with grief and nervous exhaustion to do it herself. Many of the phone calls, made from her aunt's house, had been lengthy affairs, especially to those with no prior knowledge of George Whitehead's terminal condition. Aunt and niece had regularly wept together as they carried out the tasks.

She had written a number of letters where either phone calls were inappropriate or no phone number was included in her mother's address book. The first such entry was for Adams, Don and Sandra, in the UK. She showed it to her aunt.

"Is that…?"

Her aunt looked at her with a little smile. "They're your Greg's parents," she confirmed.

"Hardly *my* Greg!" Ruth gave a tiny, protesting laugh. "After all, he was twenty-two at the time, and I wasn't even in my teens!"

"Your introduction to unrequited love!"

"Unrequited crush!"

"But that's an old address," Lou continued. "They moved a few years ago when Don was promoted. I can't remember the details. I've got their current address; we still exchange Christmas cards."

"What about Greg?" Ruth, amused to think that her schoolgirl crush could have left traces in an address book, flipped over the pages. But she was disappointed. "He isn't in here. Have you got his address?"

"No, I don't think I have. I know he moved when he got married, but we haven't kept in direct contact." Lou gave Ruth an arch look. "Why? Are you thinking of moving on from Darren? Greg's wife might object!"

"Lou! Stop it!" Greg's wife? Hearing he was getting married to whatever-her-name-was had been the worst pain ever. "No, I'm just wondering if we should let him know about Dad. I think he liked him and his terrible jokes."

"It shouldn't be necessary. His mother'll pass the news on to him."

"Yeah." Then Ruth laughed at herself. "Mom really didn't like him saying *yeah* all the time, did she? And she really hated me copying him!"

A brief interlude of lightness in their sadness followed, as Lou also laughed and they spent time recalling some of the events of Greg's brief tenure of her heart thirteen years previously. "I must have looked a right mess," Ruth said wistfully when Lou reminded her of that first attempt at wearing make-up. "You were very understanding about it."

"Ah well," her aunt said gently, "I knew something of what you were going through! I was young once, you know."

"Did you have lots of boyfriends, then?"

"Let's say I had my share before Harold came along! He got me on the rebound, Harold did." It was Lou's turn to sound wistful, and Ruth wondered if her aunt were about to reveal more, but she returned to briskness, saying, "Now, are you going to drop the Adamses a line? Or shall I?"

"I'll write them. That's fine."

A couple of days after the funeral, a letter from the UK arrived in response. It contained the conventional expressions of condolence but also a P.S. specifically for Ruth: *I wonder if you remember our son Greg (the artist) who stayed with Harold and Lou some years ago? He says that you were very artistic as well, and wonders if you kept it up. He's asked me to send his greetings and condolences too.*

Very artistic? Ruth smiled at the description. No, she couldn't in all honesty claim that. Not the *very*. At high school, she had discovered that she was no more than good, pretty good even, but not exceptional, and she hadn't kept it up to any great extent as academia and boyfriends had supervened. Perhaps the occasional sketch on holidays, but she couldn't remember when she had last done even that – possibly on that long trip she had taken with Donna after graduating. No, her talents in the art world had developed in a different direction, though occasionally she fell to wondering whether she *could* have made a go of it, triggering a bout of nostalgia.

She and Lou started the process of dealing with the will. Second only to her mother, she was a major beneficiary, and as well as a tidy lump sum, she would receive a large tranche of shares in AirConPro, the company founded by her father and uncle. Darren had already been eager to make suggestions about her inheritance. It annoyed her.

Before returning to Boston, she unearthed the Greg mementos wickerwork box from a cupboard in her old bedroom. She'd not looked at its contents for years. She gazed at the photographs her uncle had taken of her and Greg on that final evening. What a lovely, amiable-looking young man with his floppy hair and lop-sided smile. Very fanciable. Congratulations to her younger self on having such good taste, although for years she had felt no remnants of her early passion. Flicking through a hard-backed notebook in the box, she was amazed at the reams of adolescent purple prose about her undying and eternal love for him.

Also recorded in the book were a number of fantasies and daydreams, in one of which her twelve-year-old self had pictured her grown-up self as having become a *sophisticated transatlantic traveller* being met at *London Airport by my darling distant relative who will enfold me in his arms and never be distant again*. Hilarious!

She briefly considered taking the box and contents back to her tiny Boston apartment, then firmly rejected the idea. If Darren should come across it, the facetiously sarcastic comments would be unendurable. On the other hand she had no intention of disposing of it – it was, after all, a formative part of her life. One of those rites of passage, as it were, ushering in the next phase of self-awareness. She would leave it at her mother's, then, while that remained an option.

It was on her return to work at the gallery that Gilly offered her the chance of the Italian trip. Proper hands-on experience, which she had no hesitation in accepting. Her mother being well supported, by Lou and Harold as well as the local church community, she could be away for the best part of a month with a clear conscience. Italy – how thrilling! Such a vote of confidence in her.

Then Lou had asked, in some idle moment, if she had thought of stopping off in England for a few days to visit Greg? No, she hadn't, and she peremptorily dismissed the notion. Over the following few days, though, in response to one or two further catalytic comments from Lou, the idea kept returning, growing stronger and more insistent each time. Yes, it would be rather fun, she conceded. After all, he had been incredibly kind to her – not every young man would take in his stride the way he had the *gooey-eyed infatuation* (Lou's expression, delivered with a teasing smile) of a twelve-year-old girl. How lovely it would be to thank him directly, and share a laugh about it. She wrote to Greg's mother for his address. The response came quickly.

A letter to Greg himself had then been answered by return... *be lovely to see you...of course you must come and stay... Penny (my wife) and Frankie (he's 11) would love to meet you... I haven't tried to explain to them exactly how we're related as I still haven't worked it out myself! Have you?* Another exchange of letters had settled dates.

Darren had been grumpy about her being away for so long. He could come with her, he maintained, make a holiday of it. No, Darren, this was work – she'd have galleries to visit, conferences to attend, people to meet, a hefty schedule to keep. None of it involving him. No problem, he had countered, he'd be able to entertain himself during the day, and they could have the evenings together, romantic Italian evenings. No, they couldn't, because she'd have notes to write up, phone calls to make, sudden invitations to respond to and occasional early nights to grab whenever possible. Early nights, eh? He had laughed. That's more like it. No, Darren, you have a one-track mind. He grumbled that she was being unreasonable. Too bad, she insisted, that's the way it is. She wasn't his possession for him to make decisions about.

Which was how they left it. But the disagreement had raised the question for her of what to do about Darren when she returned from her trip. They had been in a relationship for nearly two years, and he was personable, easy to get on with, well-read, knowledgeable enough about art, and interesting despite his obsession with exploring caves that often saw him away for long weekends ticking another cave system off his list. He was well-set in AirConPro, where, since her father's death, he had in effect become her uncle's right-hand man. Moreover, friends treated them as a definite couple, and she herself had begun to assume that they would get married one day. And yet, and yet…a vague dissatisfaction continued to disturb her.

*

All of this had been put on ice during the Italian jaunt, but it would soon have to be defrosted, when the truth or otherwise of one of Donna's flippant observations would be tested: *Every relationship has a use-before date.* She had sighed when another of hers had fizzled out, adding *or at least a best-before date.* That may be so, Ruth thought, but the defrosting of Darren – she smiled as the image of a mammoth in a glacier obtruded itself – still lay in the future, and right now – sighing in pleasurable anticipation as the plane rumbled ever faster along the runway then began to rise above Italian soil – right now, England beckoned. And, for the duration of the flight, she had something far more engaging than the thought of extinct hairy fauna with which to amuse herself. Although one trip didn't quite make her *a sophisticated transatlantic traveller,* and Greg would hardly be enfolding her in his arms when she arrived by train at Exeter, she found it irresistible to cast herself back thirteen years and replay her pre-pubescent desires and marvel at their potency.

ii

Greg ushered Ruth from the hallway into an erratically lit room, its walls mostly hidden by paintings and posters above a number of overfull bookcases. "Penny." He waved his hand towards a figure lying on a chaise-longue against the far wall, as though presenting the main exhibit. "Penny, this is Ruth."

"Hi!" Ruth raised her hand in a greeting. "Great to meet you!"

Penny — slender, elfin-featured, a languid posture on the chaise-longue, a mass of long auburn hair draped over shoulders and a cushion or bolster behind her, artfully arranged for maximum effect — put Ruth in mind of a Victorian lady recovering from a fit of the vapours.

A Tiffany lamp, positioned behind her head on a fine antique bureau, glowed in multi-coloured brilliance. On the floor, tucked up against the chaise-longue, lay a walking stick twisted like a great length of caramelized barley sugar.

She raised an unhurried hand in response to Ruth. Her expression was neutral, as though she were about to listen to some news that she knew would bore her.

Ruth felt a flicker of discomfort. "It's really kind of you and Greg to invite me."

Penny gave a tiny sigh. "Greg said he'd like to see you again," she pronounced in an etiolated voice, letting her hand drop back onto an open book, a large hardback with a portrait of a young woman in white tulle on the cover, "so I suppose that's all right."

"You're very welcome, Ruth," Greg said authoritatively, adding to his wife, "Frankie not back yet?"

"He wouldn't appear to be."

Penny's tone implied that she considered the question to be pointless. Ruth glanced at Greg. Seemingly unperturbed, he was shrugging off his jacket. Was this his wife's habitual way of speaking? What was wrong with her, anyway? Greg had put in one of his letters that she was a dancer no longer able to dance following *the accident,* but he'd given no further details.

"Ruthie, I'll put the kettle on in a tick." Greg turned to her. "But you'd probably like to freshen up and all that? I'll show you your room."

Back in the little hallway, Ruth collected her backpack and followed Greg as he heaved her heavy suitcase up the steep flight of stairs. The walls of the stairwell were crammed with photographs, mainly in black and white, and posters, all depicting dancers, many featuring Penny. Should she know her? There was something familiar about her.

On the landing wall, facing down the stairs and fully visible as she ascended, was a large, framed explosion of colour, a poster announcing the 1976 national tour of the Freedom Dance Collective, with a long list of dates and venues. Until Greg blocked Ruth's view near the top, Penny was again easily identifiable, a dramatic pose, head flung back, right arm extended in a gesture of pleading, body and face radiating exquisite grace. The contrast with the Penny downstairs was acute.

Ruth joined Greg on the small landing lit by a skylight, its glass in need of cleaning. Of the four doors leading off the landing, only the blue one had a sign on it, announcing in black gothic script: *Frankie's Den* with *No Admittance* underneath.

"That's our room." Greg pointed at the furthest, yellow door. "Penny's and mine." He spoke loudly as if to emphasize *not yours*. Was this for Penny's benefit? "Frankie's room" – more pointing – "as you can see; bathroom" – behind the green door – "and this" – pushing open a pale pink door that stuck slightly before yielding – "is your room!"

A crowded space: bed, wardrobe, a chest of drawers, two chairs of different sizes, a bookcase containing a muddle of books and box files, and a long rack of vinyl records in their sleeves. Several shelves held a heterogenous display of ornaments and general bric-à-brac. Ruth smiled in relief that this was no beautifully tidy guest room. It belonged to the same category of cluttered rooms she was used to – her childhood bedroom, her old room at college, the bedroom in her apartment.

She went in. Greg followed and partially closed the door. "Ruthie." His voice dropped to a murmur. "Sorry about Penny; she's going through a difficult time right now and does get rather spikey. Her pain management needs tweaking again – she's got someone coming in tomorrow."

"I'm sorry it's difficult for her. Perhaps I shouldn't have—"

"Oh yes you should." He anticipated her. "I've been looking forward to seeing you – a touch of normal life for us all, having a guest to stay! Frankie's looking forward to meeting you. Anyway," as he tugged the door back open his voice returned to its louder level, "you'll find space in the two top drawers there, and some hanging space in the wardrobe. Towel for you on the chair, but if you want a bath towel look in the bathroom cupboard. Help yourself."

"I'll have a shower if that's all right."

"Ah." Greg scratched his right cheek. "I warn you that shower's a tricky devil. You have to do a lot of tap twiddling to keep the water temperature reasonably stable. I need to get the plumber in."

"Don't worry, I'll risk it!"

"I'll leave you to it. Come down when you're ready."

Greg left. As she heard him descend and re-enter the main room, Ruth sank onto the bed and closed her eyes. Was this one big mistake?

*

It had started well: it had been so lovely to see Greg waiting for her at the station, and he actually *had* given her a hug – once he had recognized her! That had been funny – she had recognized him straight away, unmistakable despite now being in his, what? Mid-thirties? Blue eyes, hair no longer floppy but cropped, and a beard! Not a substantial one by any standard, but not simply one or two days' growth. An artistic statement? Or merely the logical and inevitable outcome of a perpetual reluctance to shave? Still slightly round-shouldered, he looked somehow more substantial than she was expecting. She couldn't be sure, but had he put on weight? And he was wearing an ancient-looking tatty black leather jacket. What had happened to the bomber jacket? Curious, she realized, how you expect someone to be unchanged after many years when you haven't seen them, even to the extent of wearing the same clothes.

She had stood looking at him for several seconds as his gaze unsuccessfully scanned the throng of passengers splitting like a river delta as they came through the line of ticket barriers, before she took pity on him and, backpack on one shoulder, she trundled her suitcase towards him.

"Hi." Dumping the backpack. "*Cousin* Greg!"

"Hey! It's you! Ruthie!" He flung up his hands in a gesture of amazement, before hugging her. "You're looking good." Releasing her, he took a step back to study her, his smile, she was pleased to see, still as lop-sided as she remembered. "You've, um, grown a little since – you know!"

"Since I was twelve?" She laughed at his stumbling to finish the sentence. "I should hope so!"

"True! You're no longer a, er, a—"

"Gawky, gauche, immature pre-teen?"

"I never called you that? Did I? Surely not!"

"Of course you didn't. You were far too kind. I bet you thought it, though."

"No, I didn't!" He protested with a laugh that suggested he had thought it, maybe just a little. "You were a nice kid. Okay, let's get outta here." He wheeled her suitcase through the main exit into the outside world, nearly banging her ankle. "Right, that heap of rust over there is my car. I'll bung this in the boot – or 'trunk' as you Yanks insist on calling it."

With suitcase and backpack stowed, and her in the front passenger seat, they set off. Weird – she had gone to the wrong side of the car and wondered why Greg had laughed until she realized she was standing on the driver's side. They smiled at each other, before, with a sudden rush of happiness, she almost skipped around the car to the other side where Greg held the door open for her.

"Ma'am," he had said gravely, making her laugh again.

As they waited to swing out of the car park, the traffic was dense and slow moving. Greg drummed on the steering wheel. "Rush hour *and* poets' day."

"Really? What's that?"

"Push off early, tomorrow's Saturday. That's if you're polite. *Piss* off early, if you're not!"

Ruth laughed, happy at his mild vulgarity. "I like it!"

"Cheers!" Greg held up a hand to a driver allowing him to pull out, before asking, "How was Italy?"

"Wonderful! Fabulous! You can't imagine."

"I reckon I can, Ruthie. I had a couple of fantastic trips myself a few years back. Just magic. Where was your favourite?"

"It was all my favourite!"

"Come on – choose!"

"I guess the Uffizi was pretty special."

"Yeah, good choice, of course. But what about all the lovely little unregarded backstreet galleries, you know, where you stumble on them while hoping to get a coffee away from the crowds?"

"Oh, yes. Some real gems! Now, where was it I came across this utterly fabulous little place, where…" And she entered into a teasing competition with Greg about who had been where and seen what, and which proprietor of some tiny gallery, desperate to make a sale, had most reduced the asking price of any painting in which they had shown the remotest interest. Then all this bantering somehow segued into where the best cappuccinos could be found and an elated Ruth was laughing joyfully at it all. How easy he was to be with. How quickly they'd started chatting away and exchanging banter like lifelong friends.

All the while, their progress was no more than a crawl punctuated by complete halts along a ridiculously narrow road bordered high up to the left by a long row of houses with precipitous front gardens, and to the right by meandering iron railings keeping at bay a mass of brambles and shrubs, beyond which a river, dark and turbulent, could be glimpsed.

"Dammit! This is even worse than I was expecting." Greg broke off from the cappuccino challenge, his fingers again drumming a rhythm on the steering wheel, but his tone still light. They had left the precipitous front gardens and come to a halt behind a long line of traffic waiting at lights to cross the river.

A little ahead and off to the left, Ruth could see a long, stone, grass-covered walkway in poor repair raised on arches over a grassy dip. There was a squat tower-like structure halfway along. She pointed. "What's that? It looks rather odd."

"It's a mediaeval bridge. Well, the remains of. Thirteenth century. Once upon a time, all this would have been marshland. I don't know when it was drained."

Thirteenth century? Seven hundred years old? She knew she shouldn't be amazed. She had seen plenty of ancient buildings in Italy, and of course it was common knowledge that the States was a youngster compared to European civilization. But all the same...*seven hundred years?*

Traffic had started moving again. In fits and starts they drove over the river, through more traffic signals into a residential area, with turn-offs to stores and a gas station, soon arriving at what she knew the British called a roundabout. Greg had fallen silent, concentrating, she could tell by his tense physical posture, on driving. Then they were clear of the city limits. He relaxed. They were heading along yet another ridiculously narrow road, bordered by trees and bushes, which ran alongside an elevated and noisy highway.

"Welcome to Switham," he announced cheerfully as, turning onto a village road, they passed a war memorial, "named, it is said, after St Swithun, who didn't live here. See on the left," he took on the tones of a coach tour guide, "the village hall, venue for concerts, discos, theatrical extravaganzas, wacky exercise classes a speciality..." A few yards further on they passed a farm entrance. "An agricultural establishment offering excellent pick-your-own strawberries later in the year – the local pub, also known as a public house – like your bars – *Cheers* and all that – and here we have the Congregational church, if you ever fancy congregating – village school, Frankie went there – village shop – with post office, stamps *their* speciality..."

This was the main street they were now going up? How could *the main street* of anywhere be so narrow? Made narrower still by a line of cars parked along much of one side, such that a car at the top coming down had to wait for them, flashing its headlights. As they reached and passed the waiting car, Greg held up a hand in acknowledgement, receiving in return a raised hand acknowledging his acknowledgement. Ruth failed to stifle a laugh at the thought that it could give rise to an endless sequence of acknowledgements acknowledging acknowledgements.

"What?" said Greg as they swung round to the right.

"Oh, nothing. You English are *so* polite."

"Centuries of breeding, my dear!"

Immediately right again. An area of grass soon opened up on the left, studded with a number of stately trees. Greg brought the car to a halt in front of a row of houses, where they got out. "This is the Green, and that there" – he jerked his thumb in the direction of a grey stone building with a tower half-concealed by the trees – "is St Swithun's."

"It looks ancient!"

"Nah, it's pretty modern. Nineteenth century, that's all!"

"Hey! Stop teasing me!" But not wanting him to stop.

"You probably think anything over a hundred years old is ancient." His teasing tone continued. "The tower's older, mind you. Fifteenth century. Come on, let's get inside."

As Greg went around to the rear and opened the trunk, Ruth stared at the houses they had stopped outside. A terrace of a dozen or so. There was terraced housing in Boston, but she had not expected to see it here, outside a city. And, extraordinarily, the main street they had driven up was flanked on both sides by unbroken lines of terraced houses. Was space so much at a premium that houses couldn't stand in their own grounds, but had to be squashed together like this? It would all look positively Dickensian but for the fact that these were clearly not slums. For the most part they were attractive, well-maintained dwellings with cheerful personalities. *Cosy.*

Greg's house, however, in the middle of the terrace, had an even more squashed-in appearance, narrower than the houses on each side, as though the builders had begun constructing the terrace at both ends simultaneously and worked towards meeting in the middle, miscalculating how much space would be left. The final, central homestead had had to have its proportions reduced to fit. Ironically for the house of an artist, its paintwork was in poor condition, the original yellow of the window frames and sills displaying a mottled complexion where the bare wood was exposed. Groundsel was growing along the base of the wall, rooted it would appear in the brickwork, but the small front garden itself was spring-colour bright with neat arrays of crocuses, primroses and other flowers she didn't recognize.

"Frankie's domain." Greg waved his hand casually at the display. "Very much a budding naturalist."

*

Yet here she was, barely ten minutes later, sitting on the bed and on the verge of tears. It was plain that Greg was delighted to see her but his wife was just as plainly not. What was going on there? Oh well – Ruth wiped her eyes – if that's how it is, that's how it is. She mustn't let Penny's hostility detract from her memories of the wonderful Italian trip, or from the true welcome Greg had given her.

She stowed some of her clothes in the small chest of drawers, then opened the wardrobe. As she struggled to unhook a warped hanger from the rail, she knocked the shelf, disturbing a number of what turned out to be photographs, the larger ones in gallery-style frames, the others in neat cardboard mounts for propping on surfaces. She grabbed the two that were about to slide to the floor. One was of a little girl caught in the act of fiercely attempting to walk, her hands held from behind and above by a woman who was clearly Penny. A smiling Penny with bright eyes and sunglasses pushed up on the top of her hair. The other photograph again depicted Penny with a babe in arms, and a red-haired boy of about five – presumably Frankie – by her side, sticking his tongue out at the camera. Was the baby a younger version of the toddler? She guessed so.

Curious, she took down more of the photographs. Here was Greg with the baby. Baby in an elaborate brightly painted cot. Toddler playing with bricks. Toddler on some beach with an expanse of sea in the background. Greg with the toddler in a garden. Greg with Frankie and toddler. Penny, Greg and baby. Frankie and baby. Frankie and toddler... Every photograph featured the same child as either baby or toddler. None of her any older.

Greg hadn't mentioned any children other than Frankie, either in his letters arranging her visit or in the conversation in the car.

Shaken, and feeling she had intruded on something very private, Ruth carefully returned the photographs to the shelf.

Taking her sponge bag and towel, she slipped into the bathroom. The shower provided a welcome distraction as she sought the elusive mid-point of the controls between receiving a fierce jet of cold and feeble dribblings of scalding. A bit like life, really.

iii

Her mom had said the English kept their homes only a few degrees above freezing, but it wasn't that bad. True, the house was cooler than she was used to, but nothing like Mom's dire prognostications. All the same, away with the jeans she had travelled in, on with a denim skirt over thick woollen tights, and on with her rose-coloured sweater. Time to venture downstairs again – which triggered a mild flutter of anxiety.

Opening the door into the main room, she saw an inert Penny, still stretched out artistically on the chaise-longue, with several large cushions now cocooning her. The curtains at the strangely narrow windows had not been drawn closed, and in the gathering dusk the Tiffany lamp glowed even brighter, increasing the impression of Penny being the subject of a Victorian painting from a very minor school. The murmur of voices, one of them youthful, and the sound of running water drifted through from an adjoining room.

For a few moments she stood, looking around the room. Curiously long compared to its width, it had evidently been two rooms at some stage in the house's history, but only one of the original rooms had had a picture rail, which in the enlarged room now gave the impression of there being lengths of a wooden toy railway track stuck to the wall and leading from nowhere to nowhere. The biscuit-coloured carpet was worn in places, though in the centre of the room a circular rag rug of reds and yellows provided a cheery contrast.

Of the numerous paintings, photographs and posters of all sizes on the walls, one in particular took her immediate attention. Despite its size – covering at least half the area of the wall opposite the window – the lighting in the room rendered much of the detail difficult to make out, but it was unmistakably a painting of a water mill. *The* water mill. The *very John Constable* water mill itself from the trip to Walden Pond thirteen years ago.

It was stupendous! She approached it, stared at the horse, the stonework of the building, the water cascading out, and felt an electric thrill of discovery, banishing the flutters of anxiety. If Greg had been painting stuff like this…

A slight sigh interrupted her thoughts, drawing her attention back to the occupant of the chaise-longue. Penny's eyelids were trembling. Concerned not to wake her and get drawn into conversation, Ruth quickly slipped through the open door into the other room. A cluttered kitchen, with wooden work surfaces and too many wall cupboards, like a mouth overfull of teeth. Clearly also a knock-through of what had presumably once been a separate dining room and kitchen, again with a picture rail in the dining area ending abruptly at the joins. Just inside the door were a large oval dining table and four non-matching wooden chairs to negotiate.

The chattering of the young voice stopped as she entered, and a boy with very red, very unkempt hair looked up from a vegetable-strewn chopping board. Evidently an older version – around eleven or twelve – of the boy in the photographs upstairs.

"Hello! You must be Ruth. I'm Frankie." He stretched out the hand still clutching the knife, withdrew it as she flinched, placed the knife on the board, and again offered his hand.

Greg, at the sink, grinned at her. There was a nearly empty bottle of red wine and a half empty glass on the nearby counter.

"Hello, Frankie," she said gravely, shaking Frankie's hand.

"Daddy says you're from America."

"That's right, I am. Greg—"

"I want to go to America sometime. I'd like to go to California and see the giant redwoods. They're the largest trees in the world, you know."

"So I believe. Greg, that—"

"Their real name is *sequoia*."

"You like large trees?"

"I like all trees. I like nature."

"That's great. Greg, that painting—"

"Keep on chopping, Sunny Jim, or we'll never get finished."

"Wilco!" He resumed chopping.

"Ruthie, tea for you there." Greg pointed to a mug on the table. "Apologies for the kitsch! Or would you prefer...?" He held up and waggled the bottle.

"Tea for now, but a glass later, thanks." She picked up the mug with its mediocre portrayal of the *Fighting Temeraire* on its side. "Greg, that painting, the water mill..." But now she had managed to get his attention, she couldn't think what to say. She covered her confusion by starting to drink the tea.

"What about it?" He took up a tea towel and began drying his hands, though an ordinary blue towel lay crumpled next to the draining board.

"What about it?" Her confusion dissipated. "It's fantastic. That's what about it. You did that, what? Immediately you got back to England? In '73?"

"I started it then, yeah." He tossed the tea towel on to a work surface. "That's fine, Frankie. Put them in the steamer, could you?

Yeah, I had to do it in several concentrated bursts over months. Well, more like a couple of years."

"Is that all right, Daddy? Can I go and watch TV?"

"Twiddle the gas up a bit, then off you go. Good work."

"I want to see it in proper lighting," Ruth persisted, refusing to be thwarted by culinary considerations. "You're not doing it justice where it is now."

"You may be right." He sounded diffident. "And I guess it's your job to know that sort of thing. You like it, then?"

Hands resting on the table, she leaned forward to stare at him. "Listen to me, Greg. Seriously. It is…superb!"

"Well, Ruthie, that's quite something. You saying it. Your opinion." His characteristic crooked smile emerged and he put a hand up to his hair as though to smooth back an errant lock.

Frankie had left the kitchen, and Penny now entered, leaning heavily on her barley sugar walking stick. "You're looking pleased with yourself," she said, her tone to Greg sounding like an accusation.

"Ruth's just saying she likes the water mill." Greg repeated his hair-smoothing gesture.

"Hmm, yes. It is good." Penny's sole comment a grudging concession. "Is there any tea going? Could somebody give me some?" She lowered herself gingerly onto one of the dining chairs, partly obscuring a large poster on the wall behind her. Ruth had only just noticed it. A middle-aged man in a garish outfit and a white hat was leaning forward and gazing out of the poster with a glint in his eye and a broad smile unleashing a fine set of teeth. Across the poster was scrawled in black: *To Tommy! Now here's a funny thing! Best wishes, Max.*

"Coming up." Greg finished his glass of wine in one go, and turned his attention to tea making.

Ruth, conceding a temporary defeat, dropped the subject of the painting. Sitting down, she addressed Penny. "Have you lived here long?"

"Too long." Penny gave a fleeting grimace. The way she was sitting caused her hair to hang away from her face, revealing a long, angular white scar on her right temple. Then she shifted, and her hair once again concealed the scar.

"We moved in when we got married." Greg was wielding a bottle of milk like a chemist handling a test tube full of an unknown chemical about to be analysed.

"For a few months, it was meant to be," Penny muttered.

"It's done us pretty well," Greg countered. "It actually belongs to Penny's mother and, a spot of luck this, the tenants chose to move out just in the nick of time for us. It was Pen's grandparents' house before that. It's a bit small, but we manage fine. Don't we?" He appealed to his wife as he put a mug of tea in front of her. It depicted van Gogh's *Irises*.

"Mmm." But Penny was evidently not disposed to continue with the topic, glowering at the drink before lifting the mug to her lips. Ruth half-expected her to complain about it being too hot, or not hot enough, or the wrong strength, or in the wrong mug.

"Hey, Ruthie!" Penny's brow contracted at Greg's use of the diminutive. "I've been meaning to ask, how's your mother doing?"

*

"Steak and kidney," Greg announced, placing before her a plate containing a generous helping of pastry that failed to conceal a thick oozing of gravy. A smaller portion for Penny. Frankie had already taken his food through to the main room to watch Star Trek.

"Great. Thanks." *Steak?* she wondered. *What steak? You're not telling me there's a T-bone or ribeye hidden under all that?* "Looks good."

"Help yourselves to veg" was accompanied by the appearance of a saucepan of potatoes and a large dish of carrots and peas. "Vino?" He was again waggling a bottle. "White or...um... white? I thought we had another bot of red, but apparently not."

"Oh, in that case, I'll have white!" She laughed – not that Greg's badinage was particularly funny, but the light-heartedness was a relief. The last ten or fifteen minutes had been painful, catching up Greg on how her mom was, and Uncle Harold and Aunt Lou, and Brad, but with Penny constantly wriggling, and shifting her position, and making tiny sub-vocalizations of grunts and snuffles, which somehow sucked all the attention out of the room.

"Good choice." Greg started to pour. "Yeah sorry, it ought to be red, but let's—"

"Do get a move on." Penny pushed her glass across the table towards Greg, who hesitated momentarily before filling it. "Thank you," she said in a not-quite-sarcastic tone.

"I'm very happy with white," Ruth said as Greg filled her glass. "Thanks."

"That's lucky." He sat down, filled his own glass then raised it. "A toast to transatlantic entente!"

"Hear, hear!" Ruth raised her glass, then drank a little. "Do you remember the last evening of your visit?" she smiled at the memory. "That was the first time I was allowed to drink wine."

"And you haven't stopped since?"

"Hey! I'm very abstemious as a rule."

"*You* should cut down," Penny interrupted fiercely, adding to Ruth, "He drinks far too much. He's putting on weight."

Greg ignored the comment, asking, as they started to eat, "What are you painting these days, Ruth?"

"Oh. I, er, actually," she stammered, "I'm afraid I'm not."

Greg looked shocked. "Really? Since when?"

"Since quite a few years. I'm not good enough."

"That's a nonsense! You were great."

"No, I wasn't. I was good, I suppose, but not great. I do the occasional sketch, from time to time, but I realized the thought of trying to pursue it as my career was not very realistic. Which is why I switched direction and went in for working in a gallery. Which I love!"

"That's a hell of a shame, though." And for a few more minutes he continued to insist that she had shown great potential, possessed a lot of skill, had a terrific eye. All very flattering, but she was relieved when eventually she was able to redirect his attention to her work at the gallery and how she hoped to progress. Greg listened attentively, making regular noises of approval and delight.

Frankie wandered in with his plate and asked for seconds. "Did you know there's a bristlecone pine in California that's five thousand years old?" he solemnly asked Ruth, gazing steadily at her as though she were a tourist attraction.

"That puts mediaeval bridges in their place." Greg slapped more pie onto the plate.

Frankie returned to *Star Trek*. Greg topped up the wine glasses and suggested that the next day they could go into Exeter, "to see the sights, such as they are. Or nip down to Exmouth and see the sea if you prefer?"

"Let's do Exeter, I'd like that. There's the cathedral, isn't there?"

"Only a thousand years old, though – can't compete with bristlecone pines either."

"That'll do," she said gaily.

"You do know Vanessa's coming tomorrow?" Penny, who had remained silent throughout the preceding conversation, interjected.

"I hadn't forgotten," Greg said mildly. "That's in the afternoon. But I assumed you wouldn't want to come anyway."

"You shouldn't make assumptions."

"*Do* you want to come into Exeter? Of course you'd be welcome."

Penny's "Yes, I do" sounded like a threat.

"Okay, that'll be nice." Greg smiled. "You don't often get out. We'll go in the morning."

Ruth's anticipatory pleasure took a hit at Penny's decision. She pointed at the poster behind Penny. "Who's Max? Who's Tommy?"

"You don't know who Max Miller is?" Penny stared at her as though incredulous at such ignorance.

"Sorry. I'm afraid I've never heard of him. Should I have?"

"He was one of the greats of music hall. Greatest stand-up, certainly."

"The 'Cheeky Chappie'," Greg put in.

"*I'm* telling this," Penny retorted. Then to Ruth again, "Well known for his filthy jokes. The BBC banned him on occasions. My grandfather performed with him several times. On the same bill. Tommy Barcott." Penny's world-weariness had given way to animated interest. "He was a song-and-dance man, very good by all accounts, and that's where he met my grandmother, Sandra, Sandra Barcott as she became, who was a singer, like Marie Lloyd. Marie Lloyd?" The ironic smile returned. "You've not heard of her either, have you?"

"I can't say I have."

"I suppose you can't help being American! They toured together as Barcott and Barcott. Grandad's brother was an escapologist and illusionist, almost as good as Houdini, they said, and…"

Penny's voice grew lively and strong as she regaled Ruth with more information about other family members who had trod or were still treading the boards. This was fascinating. So, Penny could be chatty *and* interesting *and* engaging? She spoke proudly as if descended from royalty, her face transformed. Her eyes had brightened, and now Ruth could see clear hints of the gracious dancer depicted in the posters adorning the stairwell.

"What an amazing family tradition, the performing arts," Ruth commented at the end of what had become quite a tour of the music hall, then winced as Penny's demeanour abruptly changed, screwing up her eyes, making her look like a ferocious elf.

"Not for me now," she muttered harshly. One elbow on the table, she shaded her eyes with her hand.

Ruth flushed. Why did she say that? It wasn't an intended dig at Penny's inability to perform. Did Penny feel it was a deliberate reference? She looked at Greg, who made a slight but reassuring *it's-all-right* gesture before picking up the bottle of wine.

"Splash more?" he asked brightly, pouring some into Ruth's glass without waiting for an answer. "There's more in the fridge. Pen?" Penny held up her glass.

iv

"Coffee?"

"Yes, thanks."

"Pen? Usual?"

Penny, struggling to her feet, her stick as a support, did not answer.

"Pen?"

"Yes, yes! No need to ask."

"One ginger and whatsit, two coffees. With milk, Ruthie?"

"No milk, thanks."

"One white, one black. Go through, I'll join you in a minute."

Whistling, Greg filled the kettle and switched it on. Ruth started clearing the table as Penny made her painful way back to the main room.

"I'll see to that," Greg said. "You join Penny and Frankie."

"I don't mind."

"Okay, thanks. Nice to have some help for a change."

Ruth contrived to spin out table-clearing and crockery-stacking until Greg was ready with the hot drinks.

*

Star Trek had ended and a comedy was playing with a gentle laughter track. Penny had returned to her chaise-longue, and Frankie was on the settee. He beckoned frantically for Ruth to sit next to him. Greg took an armchair.

"What are we watching, Frankie?" Ruth asked, looking at a middle-aged couple in a small kitchen. The man, scruffily dressed, was explaining something to the woman in dungarees.

"That's Tom and Barbara." Frankie pointed at the screen. "They're growing vegetables and things in their garden, and they've got hens and two pigs. I think it's two pigs, isn't it, Daddy?"

"Don't forget Geraldine the goat. They're doing self-sufficiency, in Surbiton." Greg turned to Ruth. "That's an upmarket part of suburban London, where you just don't *do* self-sufficiency. It came out a few years ago. These are repeats."

"*I* want to do self-sufficiency," Frankie announced. "Don't I, Mummy?"

"You'd be very good at it, darling," Penny murmured. "Could you turn it down a little? It's a bit loud."

To Ruth it sounded fun, intriguing even, but exhaustion was now condensing on her like a soggy mist. She felt leaden. Such a long day. The flight. All the rigmarole at Heathrow. The train journey to Exeter punctuated by cryptic clues from the PA system. The alarming contrast, like behavioural chiaroscuro, between Greg's open welcome and his wife's open hostility. Dim awareness of her head hurting and eyes stinging at yet another incomprehensible announcement in an unrecognisable language or possibly an anagram heralding the train drawing into, or out of…out of…the airport clamour, a coffee machine hissing, with an airplane's engines roaring as a pilot who is and isn't Darren but also a fixed-grinned air hostess who repeatedly bangs an overhead locker as—

A shriek of laughter cuts through. She jerks upright as the dream sequence vanishes and she's sitting in a strange sitting room with a young boy next to her – it's Frankie, his name's

Frankie, he's Greg's son – hand covering his mouth, eyes wide open, staring in delight at his father, who is grinning broadly.

"That's rude!" Frankie exclaims. "He shouldn't say that, should he?"

"It's a great line!" Greg is now laughing.

Even Penny is smiling.

"But he shouldn't call her that, should he? If you called Mummy that—"

"If he called me that, he'd get my stick wrapped round his head."

"I wouldn't dare!' Greg held up both hands, palms outward towards Penny, in a facetious display of defence as he continued explaining to Frankie. "But he's not saying it nastily, he's saying it because he loves her. In affection. That's why it's funny. The shock element. Don't you go round saying it, though, young man!"

"No, all right."

"I'm afraid I missed it," Ruth admitted, now fairly awake.

"Tom called Barbara a silly bitch." Penny sighed. "Now can we—"

"Mummy! You're not allowed to say it either!"

"Barbara asked Tom if he still loves her," Greg elaborated, "and he said, 'of course I love you, you—'"

"Silly bitch!" Frankie exclaimed gleefully.

"Frankie!" But Greg was laughing again.

"I'm afraid I don't get it," Ruth said. "He called her a – what he called her. Why is that funny?"

"Because she isn't and he doesn't really think she is," Greg tried to explain.

"She's American." Penny was eye-rolling. "Americans don't do irony."

"What does that mean?" Frankie asked.

"Can we all just shut up and watch?" Penny sighed. "We're missing it."

As they all shut up and watched, Ruth briefly wondered how true it was about Americans and irony before the mist of fatigue again descended to deprive her of all cogent thought.

*

"Off you go, Frankie." Penny limply flapped a hand as the closing credits rolled. "Time for a quick bath and bed."

"Can I read in bed?"

"If you like."

Frankie went up to her. Still half-lying down, Penny hugged and kissed him awkwardly for several affectionate seconds until Frankie broke away.

"Night night, Mummy."

"Good night, darling. Sleep tight, and—"

"Don't let the bed bugs bite! Night night, Daddy."

"Good night, lovely boy." More hugging.

Frankie came and lingered uncertainly in front of Ruth. A memory surfaced of her standing awkwardly in front of Greg on the first evening of his stateside visit, and offering him a hand to shake, only for him to kiss her goodnight – or was it goodbye? Either way, he had kissed her. Should she kiss Frankie? Or would it be better not to? Frankie looked so hopeful, she couldn't resist leaning forward and kissing him on the cheek. Beaming, he left the room, turning at the door and saying, "See you in the morning!" She blew him another kiss and he darted away, his footsteps sounding rapidly on the stairs.

"You've made a hit there." Greg stretched, then stood up. "Time to do some washing up!"

Ruth struggled to her feet. She wouldn't capitulate to her fatigue. "I'll help!"

"No, no, that's fine."

"No, I'd like to."

"Yeah, okay then. Thanks."

"I'm trying to listen!" Penny broke in sharply as the next programme started.

Putting a finger to his lips and adopting a Groucho Marx walk, Greg headed for the kitchen. Ruth, stifling a laugh, followed him.

*

"I used to love *Happy Days*." Ruth turned from the sink, thrusting her thumbs into an imaginary belt, sticking out her elbows and giving a little swagger. "Fonzie was hilarious – he was…how can I put it?"

Greg laughed. "The epitome of cool?"

"That's about it." She turned back to the sink where she was washing up, while Greg dried and put away. "Brad was obsessed by him for a while. He slicked back his hair and copied his mannerisms. Dad used to tease him."

"Remember how he got fixated on my bomber jacket?"

"Oh yes, didn't he just!"

"Hullo…phone." Greg dropped his tea towel on the table. "Better get that."

"Phone!" Penny shouted, her voice bearing no trace of weariness.

"Christ, I can hear it," Greg muttered, before shouting back, "On my way!"

Not long now before she could get to bed. Ruth leaned against the edge of the worktop and gazed out of the kitchen window into the darkness of the backyard, a long, thin rectangle bordered on either side by tall fences. At the far end stood a single storey building of sorts, now barely visible except where a window was reflecting stray light. An outhouse of some sort. Why no scullery as part of the house? Why no dishwasher? But how impressive that Greg, having seen to the meal, simply took on the clearing up with no complaint. She rather liked doing such a simple chore with him. Somewhat different with Darren.

*

Noises told her Greg had returned to the main room and was talking to Penny. The tones of their voices were not amiable, but the words were indistinguishable. Further to-ing and fro-ing noises, then he re-entered the kitchen looking harassed.

"A slight change of plan. Penny's healer person is coming tomorrow morning after all, so Pen won't be able to join us for the Exeter jaunt."

"That's a pity," Ruth lied.

"She relies on Vanessa to keep her going. Hey," he brightened up, "we've done well here, nearly finished."

Soon they had fully finished, and returned to the main room where Penny was watching a chat show with her eyes closed. Greg again put a finger to his lips as they resumed their seats, but Penny's eyes opened and she reached down for her stick.

"I'm going to bed." She winced as she slowly swung her legs off the chaise-longue. "I can manage." She waved Greg away as he started to stand up again. Gathering up her book, she made painful progress to the door.

"Good night, Penny," Ruth said brightly. "Thank you."

"Mmm."

"I'll be up in a minute," Greg told Penny's retreating back, adding to Ruth, "You're welcome to stay down here, only make sure—"

"No, no; I'd like to get to bed soon. It's been a long day." She stood up. "But look, while there's the opportunity. That." She pointed at the painting on the wall. "I want to see it properly, and for you to tell me about it."

"I hardly notice it's there, these days." He joined her and they both surveyed the painting. "You recognize it?"

"Of course I do! How could I not? I remember in minute detail the day you saw it. *We* saw it. On the Walden Pond outing. Come on, put the lights on properly, and can I turn off the Tiffany?"

"Mock Tiffany, unfortunately. Tiffany-style, as they say. Wedding present from Shar – Charlotte – Penny's sister. Yeah, sure, go ahead."

A moment later, the painting was fully illuminated, one set of lights on the ceiling giving an overall wash, and a single lamp, also fixed to the ceiling, substituting for the sun. Greg shifted a high-backed chair and a standard lamp that partly obtruded into their sightline.

"It's wonderful." Ruth felt her mouth wanting to remain open in admiration, like Frankie's gape at the *stupid bitch* line. "I feel I could simply step forward and I'd be *there*. I could offer the horse a lump of sugar, hear that water whooshing out, go up and touch the walls, feel the waterwheel."

"It's not bad, is it?"

"Not bad? Not *bad*? It's utterly…words fail me. Where have you exhibited it?"

"I haven't."

"What?" A shriek almost as loud as Frankie's earlier shriek. "Why not? You must have."

Greg repeated his finger to lips gesture, then pointed to indicate upstairs. "I was going to submit it to the RA, but never did. Long story."

"Have you got others like this?" Ruth lowered her voice conspiratorially. "I mean, the sheer size is wonderful."

"This is the only one I've ever tackled on this scale."

"But you've got other paintings, haven't you? Where are they?"

"Out the back. My studio's out the back."

"Oh, that's what it is. Will you give me a guided tour? I don't mean now. Tomorrow?"

"Yeah, if you like." Greg switched the main light back on, and switched off the others. "Anyway, it's time for me to hit the hay. If you want to go up, I'll just lock up and so forth."

Why, Ruth wondered as she ascended the stairs, did he not sound more enthusiastic about the painting? Three or four times already since her arrival, he had steered the conversation away from his art. Or so it seemed. She had strong memories of him on his visit showing her his sketch pads and telling her about what he enjoyed drawing and painting, while encouraging her to *draw, draw, draw! Keep on drawing!* What had changed?

V

As she drew them, the curtains were revealed as pale blue with a William Morris pattern of strawberries and birds, cool and calming as light from a streetlamp filtered through them. Switching on the bedside light and switching off the main light, she sat on the bed, fatigue having descended again with reinforcements.

What a bizarre few hours. So good to see Greg again and he was clearly pleased to see her – such an easy, teasing rapport in the car and then when washing up. But Penny was something else again. Why all that hostility? Did she perceive her, Ruth, as a threat? *Was* she a threat? No, of course not…but was she? As for Penny's attitude towards Greg – ghastly. Amazing they still shared a bedroom.

She rose to her feet. Slowly on with pyjamas, a bathroom visit, a crawl under the duvet like Darren exploring a newly discovered cave system, and off with the bedside lamp.

*

Sleep did not come. The fatigue, shot through with Penny's antipathy, had taken her past the point of an untroubled descent into dreamland. In their exchange of letters, Greg had alluded to his wife being *rather an invalid*, but hadn't given the slightest hint that she, Ruth, would therefore be made anything other than extremely welcome. Hadn't he anticipated Penny's attitude? If he'd had any concerns about potential friction, he could simply have told her that they didn't have room to put her up in the house – in which case she could have booked a couple of nights in some hotel.

She knew nothing about the background to Greg and Penny's relationship, but then again, why should she? The first she had heard of Penny was the arrival of that letter on her thirteenth birthday. He hadn't mentioned Penny at all during his visit, at least not in her hearing. Had he told her parents? If he had, Mom would surely have prepared her for the news – or Aunt Lou? Mom would have told Aunt Lou and *she* would have said something; she was good at that sort of thing.

She sat up abruptly with a sharp spasm of remembered pain. Like an old war wound playing up after years of quiescence. Shrapnel working its way to the surface. *This is getting absurd*, she scolded herself, breathing deeply and slowly to recover. *Grow up; you're not that obsessed adolescent anymore.*

She lay down again. What had Greg told his wife about her? Penny must know about his visit to the States, even if only when her letter had arrived suggesting this visit. Wouldn't he have amused Penny, and friends like Penny's sister, with tales of being the object of a schoolgirl crush?

Noises. A click, followed by a faint creak. Opening her eyes, she saw a thin vertical line of brightness rapidly broadening. Her bedroom door was being opened.

"Daddy," a whisper, "are you still awake?" Frankie was silhouetted against the landing light.

"Frankie?"

"Oh, I forgot. Daddy usually sleeps in here."

She sat up again; that answers that – Greg had presumably moved back to the marital bed for the duration. "Is something worrying you? Bad dreams?"

"Oh no. I often wake up for a bit, and Daddy and I talk. Can I talk with you?" He advanced into the room without waiting for her answer. "Are those pyjamas?"

"They are." She pulled the duvet a little higher.

"Oh. Why are you wearing pyjamas?"

She smiled. "Don't you like them?"

He considered. "They're all right, as far as I could see. Actually, they're quite nice. But men wear pyjamas, and ladies wear nighties. Mummy does."

"Quite a lot of women do wear pyjamas as well, you know."

"Is it because you're American?"

"Maybe. I don't know what most British girls and ladies wear."

"It doesn't matter… I'm sure Mummy would lend you one of her nighties, if you like."

"No!" Ruth cried out, louder than she had intended. "I honestly don't think that would be a good idea!"

"All right. Actually, I think you look very pretty, even in pyjamas!"

"Why, thank you, Frankie!"

"Can I ask you something? I was going to ask Daddy, to see if he knew. But of course, you definitely know, don't you?" He was, as before, scrutinizing her unblinkingly, as though she were the cynosure of all right-thinking tourists.

"Do I? What is it I definitely know?" Ruth had drawn up her knees and was hugging them through the duvet. What an intriguing boy.

"Are you married?"

She gave a brief smile. That was a bit too near the bone for comfort. "No. No I'm not."

"Oh." Frankie frowned. "Have you got a boyfriend?"

She sighed. "I've been going out with someone for a while."

"Are you going to marry him?"

"Maybe. One day."

"Do you love him?" Frankie was persisting.

"That's a bit personal, Frankie! What is this?"

"If you love him, I suppose you will marry him."

"Too personal!"

"That's why people get married, isn't it? Because they love each other." He sat on the edge of the bed. "Daddy loves Mummy."

"That's lovely to hear." She yawned. His questions and comments were getting increasingly awkward. She deliberately extended the yawn for several more seconds. "Now, Frankie, I really do need to get to sleep."

"Mummy gets cross with him, though. I think it's because she can't dance anymore. She thinks it's his fault."

"Oh," Ruth said, disconcerted.

"Aha! A midnight assignation, is it?" A dressing-gown-clad Greg was leaning against the door frame, his hair mussed up.

Frankie turned to him. "It isn't midnight. It's only half past ten."

"Aha! A half past ten assignation, is it?" Greg immediately said in exactly the same genial tone of voice. "Come on, Sunny Jim." He straightened up. "Back to bed and let Ruth get some shut-eye."

"Roger. Night night." Frankie stood up.

"Goodnight, Frankie!"

"Sorry about that." Greg stepped into the room to allow Frankie to get past. "He must have forgotten you'd be in here."

"It's fine!" said Ruth. "He startled me, but honestly, no problem."

"Good, good."

She expected him to wish her good night again and leave, but he lingered, pulling at his thin beard and looking uncertain.

"I caught the last bit of what Frankie said to you." He glanced out into the landing. There came the faint click of a door being closed. "He's back in his room."

"About Penny not being able to dance?"

"That it's my fault." He stepped further into the room.

"That's not quite what—"

"Or so Penny sometimes says. When things are bad for her."

Her fog of fatigue had lifted slightly, but this was making her feel even more uncomfortable. Did she want to be the recipient of Greg's confidences? In a way, yes; who doesn't like to hear the inside story of other people's relationships when there's evidently something odd going on? But it didn't feel quite right, particularly with Penny close by.

"She's often in a lot of pain," he continued. "The pain management is very tricky."

"What happened?" She decided she did want to hear.

"Don't you know?" He sounded confused. "Sorry, I thought you did. She was in a car accident and got badly injured, which is what put paid to her dancing career."

A memory was triggered. A faint memory: a news item from some years back, in some journal on cultural matters. Penny. A dancer – Royal Ballet? Her career cut short by a car crash? Then the surname *Barcott* swam into her mind from the mealtime conversation.

"Penny *Barcott*?"

"You have heard of her?"

"We're not unenlightened in the States."

"Yeah, of course." Greg nodded. "That was her stage name – maiden name, actually. Fabulous dancer, but no longer, which, obviously, has been difficult for her to come to terms with. She hasn't, really. Come to terms with it."

He was speaking without lowering his voice, and Ruth desperately jabbed her finger in the direction of the main bedroom.

He shook his head. "It's all right, she's out for the count. Heavy dose of medication. Um, yeah. She had this accident."

"I don't remember the details – if I ever knew them. Were you driving? Is that why she says it's your fault?"

"Look, I wasn't intending on telling you now, but" – his tone of voice changed, and it sounded to Ruth as though he were quoting someone – "I've started so I'll finish." He dragged out a small chair from the corner of the room. "If that's okay?"

"Sure."

He perched on the edge of the chair. "No, I wasn't even in the car. She was driving."

"So how could it be your fault?"

"Because I should have been picking Frankie up, but I was talking to someone about a commission, so she went. She was cross *and* in a hurry, jumped some lights, and wham, another car ploughed into her. She was massively injured. It was all fucking awful."

"Oh God. I'm so sorry, Greg."

"Yeah. Thanks. I don't want to burden you, but I thought, just so you knew something of it. I was going to tell you tomorrow. There's other stuff I'll explain..." His eyes were glistening. "But not just now. Anyway, I'd be grateful if you didn't think badly of her. It's difficult for her."

"And you."

He nodded slowly. "So, anyway, I'm sorry she hasn't been exactly welcoming, but that's how it is for her, and if you could—"

"I do understand!" She had heard enough. Flattering that Greg wanted to confide in her, but what was she supposed to do with the information? "It must be really hard for everyone."

"Yeah."

He abruptly stood up, knocking over the chair. "Thanks for understanding. Anyway," he picked up the chair and returned it to the corner, "see you in the morning. We'll have a good day tomorrow. Sleep tight."

"That'll be nice. Night."

He left, closing the door quietly. She lay down again and shut her eyes, but there still nagged away at her the feeling that there was something else she had read about Penny's accident, which was refusing to unveil itself. The fog was descending once more, overcoming her attempts to retrieve the possible memory, until finally she fell asleep.

vi

When she awoke it was light outside. The curtains were unlined, and the birds and strawberries did nothing to maintain any illusion of night-time. Feeling snug, and trying to ignore a call of nature, she wondered when the others would be up and about. Would it be all right to go and have a shower? She doubted Greg and Penny had an en suite, and she shouldn't occupy the only bathroom longer than absolutely necessary.

She was no nearer to resolving the matter when there came a faint tapping of fingernails on the door.

"Hi?"

The door opened a fraction. "Ruthie, hi! How are you doing? Sleep okay?"

She yawned, considering. The fog had definitely dispersed. "Yes, I think I did, thanks. You can come in."

"Being asleep is a bit like the sixties, isn't it?" The door opened wider but Greg remained on the landing. "If you can remember it, then you can't have been there. Anyway, I'm making some tea. Want some? Or something else?"

"Tea would be lovely. Not too strong."

"Ordinary, or Earl Grey? Penny has Earl Grey first thing."

"Ordinary, thanks."

She remained lying in bed a minute or two longer, then decisively threw back the duvet, swung herself out of bed and headed for the bathroom. It really had been a surprisingly good sleep.

The mug of tea awaiting her on her return depicted Monet's *Woman With a Parasol*. It reminded her of Miss Abrams, the junior school teacher who had encouraged her art. Her range of arty aprons had introduced Ruth to many famous paintings.

Some time later she headed downstairs, where Greg and Frankie were already in the kitchen putting breakfast things on the table. Penny, Greg told her, would be having breakfast in bed – he was just getting a tray ready for her – and Ruth's sense of well-being increased a couple more notches.

*

"I know it looks like just a boring old garden shed," Greg rattled the key around in the lock of the door that led from the kitchen into the backyard, "but as you'll see, it's *two* boring old garden sheds which I put back to back. Greg 'Two Sheds' Adams, that's me."

"Neat idea." Ruth wondered how even two sheds would be big enough for an art studio.

The lock yielded. "Must get someone to fix it." Greg pushed the door open and stepped outside. "Hey, you joining us?"

Ruth turned to see Frankie behind her. He smiled at her and took the hand she offered.

"Lead on," she said to Greg, who went striding down the yard towards his studio.

The part of the yard adjoining the house was not the well-manicured lawn area she associated with English gardens but more of a homeopathic dose of wilderness consisting of rank grass dotted with undistinguished flowers. By the left-hand fence two bushes with intimidating thorns and glossy green leaves stood guard over what turned out to be a large, sunken, water-filled cast iron bath in which were growing a number of plants and reeds.

"My wildlife pond," Frankie said, tugging her towards it.

"That's really neat." She crouched down to look.

"We had frogs in it last year." Frankie knelt beside her. "Loads of 'em. That's why there are bricks in it, so they could climb out. But there haven't been any this year. I don't know why. There are newts somewhere, and we get hawker dragonflies, they're those big ones, and damsel flies. The blue ones. D'you know what the difference is between damselflies and dragonflies?"

Ruth didn't. When Frankie had finished telling her in his breathless manner, they stood up and continued towards Greg waiting at his twin sheds. The wilderness gave way to an area of heavily fissured concrete, where there stood, as well as the studio, an open-fronted shelter housing two bicycles, a clutter of spades and forks, a step ladder, lengths of wood and guttering, flowerpots, children's toys, a circular wooden table needing major surgery, and a metal contraption she supposed was a barbecue. A wooden trellis set against the garden's brick back wall supported espalier fruit trees in need of pruning.

Greg turned and waved his hand at the studio as they approached. "Voilà! Entrez!"

"Merci, m'sieur."

He pulled open the door and she was immediately confronted by a venerable piece of solid furniture in dark wood. It had numerous drawers, the brass handles of which, where they weren't actually missing, were dull and blotchy. On its top surface stood an old-fashioned pendulum clock, the case ornately carved in a lighter wood and the glass front decorated, perhaps etched, with designs straight out of Arthur Rackham. The pendulum was motionless. Clustered at the foot of the clock, like peasants petitioning a mediaeval king, were a variety of ill-matched mugs and cups and glasses, a kettle, a toaster, several bowls and plates, and an opened packet of cookies – biscuits, she corrected herself, not cookies – looking way past their best-before date. A lump of something yellow on a plate didn't look too healthy either. Ancient cheese? Cake? The remains of a once living and breathing small creature?

"Sorry about the mess!" Greg picked up a plastic box that evidently acted as a waste bin and cleared the decaying food or dead animal into it. Ruth gathered the plates and bowls onto a solitary tray.

"Feel free to wander around." He vaguely waved a hand to indicate the entire scope of his domain, then knelt and started tugging at a drawer. "I want to find an old sketch pad that'll interest you."

"The clock's stopped again, Daddy," Frankie said in a hopeful voice.

"We've been neglecting our temporal duties." Greg looked up briefly. "Why don't you wind it?"

"Wilco!" Frankie had already opened its glass front.

Ruth wandered as bidden, getting the feeling that it wasn't only clock-winding duties that had been neglected. Duties to Greg's artistic calling seemed to have been equally neglected. Occupying a long wall, under a grimy window blotched on the outside with bird droppings and, on the inside, festooned with dusty cobwebs containing remnants of dismembered flies and moths and other winged creatures, stood a table covered with all manner of pads and paper and boards, with a scattering of pencils, charcoal sticks, wax crayons, a clutch of aerosol cans, metal clips and other art materials. The table had tall lamps clamped to it, one on each side and angled on to the working surface. On top of the scattered sheets, a sketch in progress of an urban street had acquired a patina of dust.

Next to the table, an easel, where she would have expected to see a painting, or perhaps a canvas hidden from inquisitive eyes beneath an old sheet, stood empty. Beyond, lining the walls, were numerous shelves bearing an array of wooden and cardboard boxes with peeling labels on their sides, and paints in tubes and plastic bottles, brushes stiff with dried paint, well-used palettes of different sizes – all with the look of things that hadn't been moved for a long time. It was as if everything were hibernating, or simply dead. When had Greg last been in there to work, to draw, to paint, to create? It pained her to see the neglect. How she had once loved keeping all *her* art materials in regimented order.

"Shall I show you some of Daddy's pictures?" Frankie was back at her side, again taking hold of her hand. The clock was now ticking briskly, though it registered twenty past four.

"Is it all right to have a look?" Ruth asked Greg.

"Of course," he said, half-turning. "Rummage through them." He pointed to a number of free-standing racks lined up against the far wall, then continued searching through the drawers, muttering to himself.

Ruth started looking through the accumulated art: sketches, rough drafts, completed pictures, abandoned pictures, in charcoal, pencil, crayon, oil. Mainly representative art, but some abstract. They were good, but not great. Nothing like the standard of the water mill painting.

At another rack, Frankie pulled out several detailed sketches showing cartoon characters – comical birds, whimsical animals of the forest, fantasy predators in alien landscapes. "This is my favourite one," he kept saying, holding up first one then another, then another. "No, I mean this one! Do you like this one?"

"It's great!" Ruth said, mechanically. "Yes, that's good." The cartoons were good, in their way. Skilfully executed, no doubt, but she felt mildly disappointed. She supposed she had been hoping for something else, something truly special.

Further along the wall, beyond the racks, dust sheets shrouded something lumpy. She lifted one off slowly, cautiously, then another, as though not wishing to disturb hibernating animals.

Canvases. The front one, in oils, depicted three faces, all male, all laughing, dissolving into each other. Her mood switched abruptly. *This is more like it! This is* good, *I mean*, really good! She pulled it right out and found the legend, *Unholy Trinity – A.R.P. (Alex, Rob & Phil)* in the bottom right-hand corner, but no date; and this one behind it – oh wow, the depiction of a young woman, head thrown back, mouth gaping in an intense laugh. Its title was simply *The Laugh*. Then a set of four paintings of the interior of a wood with weirdly shaped oak trees growing among boulders covered in moss and lichen. More lichen positively dripped from many of the branches. One painting for each of the four seasons. Surely a place of spirits, legends and magic. What the hell was this stuff doing buried away in a make-do studio? Why wasn't it on display?

She flipped to another canvas and gasped, a violent shock jerking her back. She was confronted by the seated figure of a young girl – her identity unmistakable; the woodland in which the figure was sitting equally unmistakable. Herself, aged twelve going on thirteen, the brace on her teeth just visible, sitting on a tree stump by Walden Pond.

"That's a nice one," Frankie said solemnly, abandoning the cartoon animals and joining her. "I don't think I've seen it before. Who is she?"

She controlled her breathing with an effort, and glanced round. Greg had found what he was looking for in the drawer, and was now flipping through a small pile of sketch pads. "Who knows," she said to Frankie in a quavering voice. "You'd better ask your dad."

"What's that on her teeth?"

"I think it's a brace." Still quavering.

"Oh yes, I know. If you've got wonky teeth. She's sort of pretty," he added in a doubtful tone of voice.

Sort of? She nearly laughed out loud. *Sort of pretty! That's kind of you, Frankie!* No, not pretty. Gawky, she'd say. She'd definitely been a gawky twelve-year-old. Where was the signature? *Gregory Adams*. Beside it: *RW, Walden, May 1973*.

Cautiously, she tilted the canvas forward, revealing the one stacked behind it. A second shock. Same location. Same figure – only it wasn't. *This* RW held an identical pose, but with a more mature body shape, the face more filled out, no brace! Then on a third canvas, another imagined RW, several more years on, now with a stunning coiffure, far better than her hair had ever been, and wearing what was surely a prom dress, with a hint of decolletage. Attached to her dress, a corsage of three blue flowers, matching the figure's eye shadow.

"Found it." Greg sounded triumphant. "Never throw anything away. I've got the original sketches of the water mill. Do you want…oh bloody hell!" He was right behind her.

"Language," said Frankie.

Ruth turned. Greg, a hand on the back of his neck, a look of great embarrassment on his reddening face, stared at the painting. She turned back and continued to study it, her mind in a tangle, not knowing what to say. Behind her, Greg, too, still seemed to be having difficulty with speech.

Only Frankie was not at a loss. "Isn't she *pretty*, Daddy?" he said. "Was she one of your girlfriends before you met Mummy?"

vii

"Can I ask you now?" Ruth said. "What gives with those paintings of me? Or based on me?"

Greg's response when she had asked him back in the house had been a dismissive wave of the hand and "Later, Ruthie. Tell you later."

The car juddered as he made a maladroit gear change. Did all British cars, she wondered, have such old-fashioned mechanisms? Hadn't they heard of automatics? They were heading into Exeter, just the two of them. Frankie had been desperate to join them, but Greg had insisted he join his regular Saturday morning Junior Foresters' outing.

"Yeah," Greg said slowly, in response to her question. "I should have hidden them somewhere."

"Well, you didn't! Come on, explain."

"Don't worry," defensively, "it's nothing dodgy. I'm no weirdo."

"I should hope not! I was only twelve at the time."

"I know that. But do you remember I told you that day we all went to Walden you had an interesting face, and—"

"Actually," she interrupted, then paused, wondering whether to continue. It seemed a trivial point, but it had been of intense importance to her twelve-year-old self.

"Actually what?" Greg executed another, smoother gear change as they approached the roundabout.

"You didn't say that about my face when we were at Walden."

"No?"

"No. You'd said it earlier, when you all came to our house that evening and I'd been looking at your sketchbook. You drew me then, saying my face was interesting, *and* you wanted to add my nose to your collection!"

Greg laughed and banged on the steering wheel several times, then braked sharply as a lorry lumbered past them on the roundabout and from the right, surprising her. "Your *nose*? I don't remember *that*." They were on the move again.

"My nose! You had a page of noses in your sketchbook and you drew mine as well, to add to them. That was when you said I had an interesting face."

"Yeah, you're right. I was collecting noses. You have quite a memory."

Ruth nodded. Yes, she did have quite a memory – for some things. Her younger self, she had discovered, didn't just vanish as she grew up; it left behind islands, albeit often unseen, submerged, of enduring emotions. Greg's visit of thirteen years ago had caused an entire archipelago to form, erupting from the ocean floor. She now had an uncomfortable but indefinable sense of further movement taking place in the depths.

"Anyway," Greg continued, "wherever I said it and whenever I said it, I meant it. What's more, you *still* have an interesting face. After I'd done that sketch at Walden, when I got back here, I used it as the basis for the painting you saw—"

"There are *three* of them!"

"Four."

"Four?!"

"Let me explain. I used the sketch as the basis for the *first* painting, obviously, which I thought would be a one-off, but then

I got to wondering how your face would change, or develop rather, as you got older. You know Rembrandt's series of self-portraits?"

"Sure."

"I had this idea of creating an analogous time sequence of imagined changes in someone as they got older. You. So, I painted the second one, imagining you three years older, then another with you on what I suppose you'd call the cusp of womanhood, and I painted a fourth, which you didn't see. It's not in the studio. Phil's got it on long-term loan. He was very taken with it."

Now that *is* weird, an image of a future version of herself hanging on some stranger's wall? She felt a slight fluttering in her stomach, as though waiting to be called in for an important interview. "I don't know whether to be flattered or not," she said.

"Hey, I hope that's not offended you?" Greg sounded worried. "I was—"

"No, you haven't. Not at all! I just… Well, I don't know what to say. But I thought they looked good – no, let's be honest: they looked fabulous! I didn't exactly see them in the best of conditions and for not that long – I couldn't examine them. But I could see their quality straight away. So, Greg!" She couldn't keep the excitement from her voice. "What the hell are they doing stuck there in your studio? Along with the others, like the three guys' faces merging into one—"

"Phil, Rob and Alex. That's from years back, doing their comedy. I was at school with Phil and Rob."

"They should be out in the world as well, as should the water mill, and those of some weird forest, right out of Tolkien or something. Them too."

"Wistman's Wood. Yeah, I did quite a lot of them once. Had prints made, too – they're pretty popular. They sold well. I ought to get another batch of prints done. We could do with the dosh."

"At least you're doing *something* with them – but haven't you ever exhibited them? Any of them?"

"No, no, I haven't."

"Why, Greg? Why haven't you?"

"It's a bit of a story, that. All to do with the accident, you see. Penny's accident. I've not been sure how much to tell you, but maybe I do need to let you know it all. Can it wait till we've got a coffee?"

*

The chilly start to the day had given way to a warm spring morning, and they sat outside the Café Leofric in Cathedral Close. In the short but meandering walk from the multistorey car park Greg had already pointed out some of the historic buildings: the Guildhall, some mediaeval churches, a short stretch of the old Roman wall.

The young, tattooed waitress had placed their coffees and croissants on the table and retreated. From where she was sitting, Ruth could see not only the great cathedral to her right but also another mediaeval church, tiny, in reddish stone, in one corner of the Close, next to a second tea shop. Under the grass of Cathedral Close itself, Greg had told her, right in front of the cathedral's west end, were the remains of Roman baths. She felt dizzy sitting in the presence of so much history.

There was a silence between them. Greg had tipped several sachets of sugar into his coffee and was stirring it slowly. Ruth broke a piece off her croissant and chewed it as she gazed across at the cathedral. A magnificent structure, if not quite up to San Marco's, providing a terrific backdrop. Cathedral Green was buzzing with activity.

"Frankly, the accident was a life-changer," Greg's voice broke in.

Ruth turned her attention from the cathedral back to Greg.

"Not in a good way. Obviously. As I told you, it wrecked Penny's health and career, but that's not the half of it." His eyes glistened. Ruth occupied herself with slowly drinking some coffee and eating more croissant, deliberately not commenting on his incipient tears.

"There was Lucy, you see," Greg said abruptly. "She was in the car at the time."

"Lucy?"

"Our daughter. Three years old. So adorable."

"Oh, Greg." Ruth put a hand to her mouth. "Was she…" She couldn't bring herself to say the word.

Greg nodded. "She was in one of these children's seats in the back, strapped in and all that. The other car hit Penny's car side on, the side where she was. Killed instantly."

"Oh, Greg," Ruth repeated. "I'm so sorry. I… I came across some photographs in the wardrobe, is that—"

"Yes. Yeah. We usually have one or two of them out in that room. Penny finds it too painful to see them around every day in the rest of the house, but I, you know, I like to be able to see her."

"Sure."

"We're talking three years ago, a bit over, but her loss is a permanent ache. She's still here, of course," he tapped the left-hand side of his chest, "but that's little comfort."

"No."

Seeing him pick up a serviette to dab at his eyes, Ruth again looked away, telling herself to give him a moment's privacy and not make any crass comment. He was emanating pain as though he were radioactive.

In a prosaic, matter-of-fact way, he went on to recount more details of the accident and its aftermath: Lucy's funeral,

Penny's months of convalescence, the police investigation, the threat, eventually lifted, of prosecution, Greg taking on the entirety of running the household and looking after Frankie. Feelings of guilt and regrets, recriminations from Penny towards Greg, recriminations from Greg towards Penny, a truce, a reconciliation… "Of sorts," he added.

Part way through the account, the waitress returned to ask, "Is everything all right?" which Ruth mistakenly took for a sensitive query about the customers' well-being. She started to reply, but Greg interrupted her.

"Yeah. Two more, I think." He looked at Ruth, raising his eyebrows. She nodded. "Yeah, we need the caffeine," he confirmed. "Thanks." The waitress gathered up their empty cups and crumb-laden plates.

"All totally ghastly," Greg summed up a few minutes later, after the second coffees had arrived. "You asked why I hadn't exhibited any of those paintings. The truth is, I've not even done any more painting to speak of since then. Not just because there were too many other things that needed to be done – though that was true – but I've just felt blocked most of the time since the accident. Grief, mainly."

Ruth managed to stop herself from saying again how sorry she was. Nodding, she remained silent.

"I do get myself into the studio from time to time, but can't get going on new stuff except for little bits and pieces," Greg continued, "like those cartoons for Frankie, and that's been good for him. I did eventually manage to finish a couple of commissions I was halfway through, and I've done one or two other really trivial things, but nothing significant. Designed some theatre posters for Tredders – he's the loony producer of local am dram. But you've seen my alleged studio – it's more like a ghost town.

"Every time I try to get down to painting something that'll mean something, I freeze. What the hell do I think I'm doing when Penny can't dance anymore, and Lucy is…that sort of feeling. Penny's not exactly encouraging, either. I'm no psychologist, but I sometimes wonder if she resents the fact that I *could* resume painting but she can't resume dancing. If I really fired up and got going again, it'd emphasize her condition. Anyway, however much I might paint, if I could paint again, it's not going to bring Lucy back, is it? It's not going to restore Penny to health and happiness. Mind you." He sighed. "I don't deny it would help the bank balance if I got my mojo back and did some saleable stuff. Though the truth is that I have so far, in my entire life, other than stuff done on commission, sold a grand total of two paintings."

"One more than van Gogh."

"True. If we believe that story. Neither of my sales were to my brother, either."

"I didn't know you had a brother."

"I don't, which is why he hasn't bought any of my paintings, the bastard."

The facetiousness briefly lifted the mood. Greg continued, "I do run a number of adult education-type painting classes, which pays reasonably well, and I can cope with it as it's not me being creative but encouraging other people to get in touch with their *inner artist*." He laughed scornfully. "I sometimes think I ought to get in touch with my inner stockbroker or inner CEO of a merchant bank. Be a damned sight more profitable."

"Can I ask you something?" she ventured, after a brief silence.

He looked enquiringly at her, again practising eyebrow-levitation.

"Going up your stairs, there's all those photos of Penny, and the posters with her on them."

"Yeah."

"But I don't think there are any paintings of her that you would have done. Or drawings. Are there?"

"No. There aren't." His peremptory tone didn't invite further enquiry. But a few seconds later he shrugged, saying, "It's not really a secret. Just painful."

"Don't if you don't want—"

"No, I'd like you to know. It's important. As you've guessed, I'd done a lot of her as a dancer, mainly little drawings, sketches, lots of them, but several really good paintings as well. She, er." He shrugged again. "She made me destroy them. Slaughter of the innocents."

"What! Why?"

"She said that Penny the dancer had died, and so my paintings of her as a dancer ought to die as well. She's always had slightly weird beliefs."

"It must have been horrible for you."

He nodded slowly. "She's all right with the photos, and the posters, though. I don't know why. I can't see the logic, but then why should there be logic? Logic doesn't rule emotion, does it? The heart has its reasons, and all that."

"You did what she wanted? Destroyed all your pictures of her?"

He did not nod but stared up at the sky for long seconds, then very slowly lowered his head, returning his attention to her. "Not quite."

"Oh."

"Not quite, to the tune of four. There are three little drawings. Exquisite, though I say it myself. I just couldn't destroy them. They're hidden securely away. As is a painting I'd virtually finished, based on a series of photographs I'd taken of her in full flow. I told myself that it didn't fall into her wholesale condemnation because she didn't know about it."

"She doesn't know about any of them, then."

"Nope. I swore I'd destroyed everything. I lied to her. I kidded myself I was doing it because she might be grateful one day that I'd kept them – but that's just self-deception. Actually, it's not really *self*-deception, because I wasn't deceiving myself. I knew all the time I was doing it for me. Me as an artist as well as me as a husband. What does that make me, Ruthie?"

"Someone who's committed to the higher truth of art, I'd say."

"Maybe…maybe."

For some time, she had been aware of tears trickling down her cheeks, but now, when she tried to wipe them away surreptitiously, Greg reached across the table and gripped her arm.

"Hey," he said. "I'm sorry it's been such a grim story."

"I'm glad you told me. Thank you for trusting me. I wish I could do something, but I can't see what."

"You've listened. I can genuinely thank you for that."

She wiped her eyes with her free hand, and sniffed. "Do you think you'll ever find your way back to painting as a way of, I don't know, working this through? Expressing your feelings? Processing it? I don't know what the right term is, or even if there is one."

"Who knows, Ruthie. Who knows."

"But even if you don't, you seriously have a fabulous treasure trove of what you've already painted. Why don't you focus on that? Exhibit what you have. Let other people appreciate it. Be proud of what you've done."

"And earn some dosh? Maybe, maybe," he repeated, removing his hand from her arm and holding it up, palm towards her. She sensed not only that she mustn't press him any further, but also that further tremors were rising from her own ocean floor.

"I think that's enough nagging from me." She drained her cup. "Now, to change the subject, I don't know what plans you have, if any, for tonight's meal, but I'd like to cook something, if that's not treading on any toes."

"Woo, nice offer." Greg arched his back and stretched his arms as though waking himself up from a deep sleep, his whole demeanour reverting to light-heartedness. "I was going to put a chicken in the oven, unless it fights back."

"I could see to all that, or I will say that I do a pretty mean spag bol."

"Oh, do you? Frankie will love you forever. Mind you, I think he already does! Okay then, you're on. Thanks. Frankie and I can be joint sous-chefs."

"Great."

"Now, how about a spot of culture, architectural division, subsection sacred?" He signalled to the waitress for the bill. "Namely, the cathedral. Then there's a place I know that does decent lunches. Proper English pub, to continue your education on the English. Yeah?"

"Yeah."

viii

The cathedral, lunch at a pub called the White Hart, a leisurely tour of the Maritime Museum, a short stroll along the river, tea in a nearby café, then back to the car and back to Switham, stopping off at the village shop for her to buy – she insisted on paying – the wherewithal for the *mean spag bol* and a bottle of red wine, with Greg buying a second bottle, saying, "Don't want to run out again!" – all the while chatting easily. This, though her feet were beginning to complain, must be one of her happiest days ever.

When they drew up outside the house, Frankie came running from the Green and opened the car door for Ruth.

"Why, thank you, Frankie." She clambered out somewhat inelegantly. "Quite the young gentleman. Would you like to bring the shopping in for me?"

"All right."

"Are you playing soccer?" She nodded towards three other boys, one of whom was holding the ball.

"Just kicking it around."

"My brother's keen on soccer, but I can't remember who he follows."

"Man United," Greg put in. "At least, he used to. See, you're not the only one with a good memory! Frankie's an Arsenal fan, aren't you? Who's that player you like?"

"Tony Adams. He's really good. Shall I take that one?" He beamed as Ruth handed him the bag she was holding, then waved to his friends, calling out, "I've got to go in now. Ruth's back."

One of the boys put his fingers in his mouth, whistling loudly. It sounded derisive. Recalling the teasing she had received from Donna, she hoped she wasn't making it difficult for Frankie. But he responded by thumbing his nose and waggling his fingers at his friends.

Greg retrieved the other bag from the back seat and kicked the car door shut. They entered the house.

Penny was in the main room, again occupying the chaise-longue, newspaper on her lap. This time, Ruth couldn't help thinking she had more than a passing resemblance to a Parisian courtesan about to welcome an eminent duke or count. Her hair again looked artfully arranged.

"Shopping?" She sounded far more relaxed and affable than formerly.

"Ruth's offered to do the evening meal."

"That's kind. What are you treating us to?"

"Spag bol."

"Hey, great!" Frankie jiggled the bag. "I love spag bol."

"That'd be nice," Penny said. "Thank you."

"Why don't you take the bag through to the kitchen, Frankie, and put the kettle on for us, please."

"Wilco."

Greg dropped into a chair next to Penny, and eased off his shoes. "How was it with Vanessa?" His tone was solicitous.

"Good." Penny's voice now sounded stronger, almost seductive. Was she making a not-so-subtle claim on Greg? "It's always good with her. She's the only one who's able to make a difference, so I've decided I'm going to ask her to come every other week from now on. I need that level of input from her."

"Hmm, right. Bit pricey."

"I'm worth it, aren't it?" She made a moue, simultaneously flicking at her hair with one hand, strengthening the resemblance to a courtesan knowing her client's particular desires.

"Yeah, sure, of course you are. We'll manage. But I think she should offer you a discount for bulk buying… I'll make some tea."

Sitting down as Greg disappeared into the kitchen, Ruth asked Penny, "What does Vanessa do?"

"Do you know anything about acupuncture?"

"Not really. Not how it works, but I know it involves needles."

"That's about all anyone knows." Penny's weary voice had returned. "But yes, special needles to stimulate the meridians – I suppose you don't know what they are either—"

"Sounds fascinating," *and painful.*

"—and she does relaxation as well, like hypnotherapy. It's what I need." Without disturbing her newspaper, Penny started flapping a hand over the side of the chaise-longue, not quite touching the floor. "I've got something for you. Can you see a book down there?"

"I'll get it." Stepping across to the chaise-longue, Ruth picked up a fat paperback with a garish cover. Its spine was marred with streaks of white where it was in danger of splitting. She held it out to Penny, who waved it away.

"No, it's for you to look at. It's about the music hall. My grandfather gets several mentions in it. Tommy Barcott. There's a lot on Max Miller."

"That's really kind of you." Ruth returned to her chair and studied the cover, a montage of brightly coloured pictures of, she assumed, stars of the music hall. "I'm sorry if yesterday I—"

"Don't." Penny stopped her with another wave of her hand. "I hope you find it interesting."

Taking the hint, Ruth opened the book and turned to the introduction. A few minutes later, Greg came in with the tea tray, followed by Frankie bearing cake.

*

"Pen." Greg sounded cautious. A second round of tea had been distributed. Ruth was still flicking through the paperback, and Frankie, reading a wildlife magazine, was talking silently to himself.

Penny put down her newspaper.

"Ruth's been pushing me to get my act together, to do something with my *portfolio*." Greg put on an ironical tone. "I think she's right, and um – I didn't tell you this, Ruth – there'll be the Devon Open Studios in September. It's an annual thing. Pretty well promoted. I'm going to see about taking part."

Penny pulled a face of disgust. "A load of strangers tramping through the house!"

"They could come up the alleyway."

"Past all the bins? How very salubrious."

"Through the house, then. It won't be that disruptive, and would be really helpful. I'll have to register pronto though. Devon Open Studios," he turned to Ruth, "is when artists and printmakers and potters and everyone opens up their studios for the gen public—"

"Hoi polloi, with muddy boots," Penny corrected.

"—to come and see what we get up to, and, with luck, buy something. Usually only a postcard or two, but you never know."

"I know the idea. I think it's great."

"I did it for a couple of years, before...well, a few years back. That's when I made my two sales."

"It'll be fantastic! Do it."

"Another thing." Greg turned back to Penny. "We were thinking... *I* was thinking," he corrected himself, "I could get another batch of prints made of my Dartmoor stuff—"

"Postcards," Ruth added.

"The postcards, yeah, and other stuff."

"T-shirts," Frankie piped up. "You could print some of those cartoons on T-shirts."

"That's an idea."

"You might not have enough room out there," Ruth said, "and since *that* is in here," she pointed to the water mill, "why not have a display in here? A mini-exhibition?"

"Excellent!"

"I'll move out," Penny said sarcastically. Affability in total freefall.

"Yeah, I know it could be exhausting for you. Maybe go and stay with Shar and Jimmy? For the week or however long. They'd love to have you."

"You haven't got enough to make it worthwhile, have you? You've not done anything worth talking about for years."

"I've got my Dartmoors, a whole heap of portraits, seascapes, the river paintings, those I did in Scotland and the Lakes... masses!"

"The pretty lady," Frankie blurted out. "You must have the pretty lady."

A pause button had been pressed. No sound, no movement, no breathing, before, "What pretty lady?" Penny demanded suspiciously.

"One of my portraits," Greg said blandly. "You've seen it. You said you liked it."

"When?"

"Well, I can't give you an exact date, can I?" Greg sounded exasperated. "Around the same time that I was doing that." He jerked his thumb towards the water mill.

"Your American trip." Penny turned and glared at Ruth. "Do you know anything about this? He was staying with your family, wasn't he?"

Feeling paralysed, Ruth could barely give even a minimal nod. What the hell was Penny getting in a lather about?

"Christ, Penny." Greg spoke with a slowness that suggested he was struggling to keep from bursting out in anger. "Of course Ruth knows about it; she was the bloody subject. I told you at the time. Walden Pond."

"I don't remember it."

"Whether or not you remember it is beside the point. At Walden Pond I made a sketch of Ruth, which I then worked up into a painting, and developed three more to go with it. I showed them to you. All of them. Phil's got one of them now, down in Kent, and the other three are out there still, in the studio."

"Oh, are *you* the pretty lady?" Frankie exclaimed. His magazine had fallen, forgotten, to the floor. "Daddy, is Ruth the pretty lady?"

Greg nodded.

"Not a very good likeness, then," Penny's voice was cold, "if Frankie didn't recognize her."

Another brief press of the pause button, then Ruth stood up. "I think I'll start doing the food," she announced, as if nothing of significance was happening. "Come on, Frankie, you're my second-in-command if you like."

Frankie leaped up.

"There's a radio out there," Greg gave her a meaningful, wide-eyed look, "if you want to listen to some music."

ix

"Can I put Radio 1 on?" Frankie looked at her hopefully.

"What's Radio 1?" Making sure the kitchen door was fully closed, Ruth went to wash her hands at the sink.

"It's got pop music. I like it. Richard Skinner's on it."

"Who's he?"

"He's a disc jockey. They play records. He does *Top of the Pops* sometimes. Daddy watches that. I think he likes the dancers. I think Mummy sort of likes it as well, but usually pretends not to."

"Put it on, it sounds good." Raised voices reached her through the wall. With any luck, it should mask them. 'Manic Monday' blasted out. "Hey, this is a good one!" She returned to the table to sort through the shopping.

"You know it?" Frankie sounded impressed. "Daddy likes them as well. Shall I open the door so he can hear it?"

"No." Luckily, she was between him and the door. "He and your mom are talking. Let's get on with the food."

"Roger."

"What would you like to do?"

"I'm good at chopping things."

"That's neat. How about you chop the onions, then?"

Frankie pulled a face. "Onions make my eyes sting."

"I'll do them, then. You could chop up some mushrooms."

"Wilco."

"Have you washed your hands?"

Frankie examined them. "Um. Sort of."

"Sort of?"

"All right." He smiled his capitulation to adult authority. "I'll wash them again."

"You chop over there by the sink. I'll use the table." She handed him the bag of mushrooms.

After the Bangles and the between-records chat, the DJ announced a track she didn't know, but Frankie yelped in delight as it started. "It's 'The Young Ones'! They do a funny programme on the telly. I'm not usually allowed to watch it because Daddy says they're rude, but Mummy lets me stay up and see it sometimes if Daddy's out teaching. That's Cliff Richard singing with them. Mummy said she used to be in love with Cliff Richard when she was a girl."

"Who's Cliff Richard?"

"He's a pop star. Mummy says girls used to go potty over him."

"Like David Cassidy?"

"Who?"

"Never mind!"

With Frankie chatting away, Ruth deliberately took her time over preparing the food, not wanting to intrude on Greg and Penny. Between records it was possible to hear that a conversation, occasionally with raised voices, was under way in the adjoining room, but the words were indistinguishable.

*

The Bolognese sauce was simmering in the saucepan. Ruth tasted it. Bland.

"Frankie, any idea if there's a spice rack or something anywhere?"

Frankie had been jigging round the room to the music. He came to a stop. "D'you mean little bottles? In one of those drawers, I think."

"Neat." She pulled open first one then another of the drawers he pointed to and found an array of little jars, their metal caps naming the contents. She took out cinnamon.

"Ruth." Frankie resumed his jigging. "Why do you say *neat*?"

"Do I?"

"You said it just now. Twice. And you said my pond is *really neat*."

"She says neat because she's an American," said Greg, coming into the kitchen.

"Do all Americans say neat?"

"When we like something," Ruth said. "Now, why don't you measure out the spaghetti."

"Neat," said Frankie.

"Fancy a pre-prandial snifter?" Greg picked up one of the bottles of red wine.

"A what?"

"Glass of vino before we eat. I'm having the red, but there's white in the fridge."

"I'll go with red, thanks. What does Penny have?"

"Oh, she'll be having a fancy non-alcoholic *beverage*," he stressed the word sardonically, "as per new instructions just received from Vanessa."

As he handed Ruth a glass, she adopted what she hoped was an interrogative expression, tilting her head in the direction of the main room. Greg gave a discreet hand waggle and mouthed *it'll be okay*.

Frankie was still jigging to the music.

*

The first taste told her something was wrong. Hot. Spicy hot. Definitely not as Bolognese sauce should be. Penny gave a loud exclamation and spat it out. Greg went "Woohoo!" and started waving his hand in front of his mouth before swallowing two or three mouthfuls of water; and Frankie, having been allowed to eat with them after intense pleading, proclaimed, "Hey, neat! I like this!" and dug in delightedly.

"Interesting," Greg said, wiping his mouth with the back of his hand. "What have you put in it? Tastes like chilli."

"Cinnamon," Ruth said defensively. "I often do. I tasted it part way through, decided it was too bland, so put in cinnamon."

"Where did you find it?" Greg asked.

"In the jar marked *cinnamon*."

"I was afraid you were going to say that." Greg stroked his beard. "Logical, but I'm afraid the lids don't always get put back on the right jars. Mea culpa. I reckon you've put chilli powder in."

"So, I should have chosen the jar marked 'chilli' to find the cinnamon?"

"That's probably paprika. Or ginger. Or soap powder – just kidding!"

"I've told you lots of times you should be more careful," Penny snapped. This was her first utterance since Ruth had called them into the kitchen.

Greg held up an apologetic hand. "Let's forget it's meant to be Bolognese sauce and think of it as chilli con carne minus kidney beans and plus spaghetti! Then it's damned good."

"Language," Frankie said.

"Which I shouldn't eat." Penny turned to Ruth. "You weren't to know. Vanessa says spicy food plays havoc with my meridians."

Her hair was disordered. She hooked one tress behind an ear, revealing the bobbly white scar.

"I'm so sorry."

"That's all right. Not your fault. Greg treats the kitchen like he treats his studio."

"Well, I think it's neat," Frankie offered.

"I'll get you something else, Pen," Greg said, half-rising.

"Don't bother!" She grabbed her stick and heaved herself to her feet. "I'll get something myself. And, Frankie, don't say *neat*. We're English."

*

For the next twenty minutes, Penny was a houmous-and-salad-eating spectre at the feast, Frankie chattered away, Greg made occasional trivial comments about their Exeter trip, and Ruth could think of nothing at all to say. This was agony. How could she get away? Escape upstairs? Disappear like they do on *Star Trek* and reappear in Boston? She felt responsible for the evident stand-off between Greg and Penny, but what had she done wrong? It wasn't of her making.

Greg was saying something. "…or down to Exmouth," he concluded. "The sea."

"Sorry, what was that? I was miles away."

"As is Exmouth, but not *that* many. Tomorrow, I was wondering if you'd like to go for a riverside walk at Steps Bridge, or go and see the sea at Exmouth."

"Steps Bridge, can we go to Steps Bridge?" Frankie begged. "Please. It's ever so good, Ruth. You'll like it. I can show you lots of things."

"Hey, Sunshine, Ruth might prefer to see the sea. Pen, what do you think? You like getting down to the sea."

Penny glowered and said nothing.

"Come on, Pen, you like Steps Bridge as well, as long as we're careful."

"Your choice. Leave me out of it."

Greg gave a slight, despairing shake of his head and slapped his hand on the table.

"Don't *do* that," Penny snapped. "You know it's irritating. I think you do it on purpose."

"Steps Bridge, *please*," Frankie repeated. "You'll come, Mummy, won't you?"

"I'll see how I'm feeling, darling," Penny muttered, smiling briefly at her son. "Your father and her," briefly glaring at Ruth, "will decide where you're going. Right now, I'm going upstairs. Someone bring me a camomile tea."

After refilling her glass and telling Ruth to go and relax in the main room, Greg said he and Frankie would make Penny's camomile tea and do the clearing up.

"I'm so sorry about the chilli."

"Seriously, don't worry. It's how great new dishes are created. You liked it, didn't you, young man?"

"It was neat."

Greg did not correct him.

*

When Greg and Frankie joined Ruth in the sitting room, they watched a wildlife programme. Frankie begged Ruth to come and sit next to him on the settee, and when she did, he pressed against her, reminding her of her own twelve-year-old behaviour towards Greg. As the programme continued, he randomly exclaimed "Neat!" and explained to her other details about the habits of bats and other cave-dwelling creatures, which, reminding her of Darren, made her suppress a reluctant giggle. She maintained an air of ignorance, which encouraged Frankie to further explanations as he cuddled up to her. Greg appeared absorbed in his own thoughts – gloomy ones, if his demeanour was anything to go by.

When the programme finished, Greg suggested to Frankie that it was his bedtime.

"Oh please! A bit longer!" Frankie sounded desperate. "I want to stay with Ruth!"

"Ten more minutes," said Greg with a glimmer of a smile. "If that's okay with Ruth?"

"Of course it is! You could make it quarter of an hour!" She felt her admirer relax against her. Again, Greg gave a glimmer of a smile.

"About Steps Bridge, tomorrow," he said, "if we go. It's in Dartmoor National Park, but I'm afraid it's not all wild and rugged. It's not exactly a Walden Pond, but it's a lovely walk along the river, not too demanding. It's a place Penny likes. Good tea shop nearby, too."

"Is she able to walk far?"

"Yeah, not bad. She'll use her stick, obviously, and it's on the level. That is, if you ignore tree roots and stuff. And there are various places to sit along the way. If she doesn't want to go far, we can walk on."

"It's neat!" Frankie was yawning.

Ruth laughed. "You like that word, don't you?"

"It's a neat word." He yawned some more, and Ruth laughed again. He seemed to be trying to burrow into her and, after a moment's hesitation, she put an arm around him. Within seconds he was asleep. How her young self had longed for something like that with Greg.

"That sounds like a nice idea," she said quietly to Greg. "I feel uneasy about Penny getting left out."

Greg nodded. "I include her when I can. Often, though, it's just not possible. It'll do her good to get out, see the daffodils, air in her lungs." He sighed and shook his head, looking glum. "I sometimes think her condition is exacerbated by all the treatment she gets, you know. And that straightforward being in the sun, and out in nature, and taking an interest would do her a lot more good. I'm really not happy about Vanessa's involvement, but it's what Penny wants. Anyway," he stood up, "I think this young fellow had better be getting to bed before he's completely immovable. I'll see how Penny is as well. I'll be a few minutes."

As Greg lifted up his son, Ruth whispered, "See you in the morning, Frankie. Kiss, kiss."

"Night night," Frankie murmured.

*

"He's really got a thing about you," Greg said, returning. "Thanks for putting up with him."

"No problem!" Sitting as she was on the settee, she leaned forward, hands grasped in front of her. Greg was back in his chair. She noticed his dark green sweater had little brown marks on it where strands of sauce-laden spaghetti must have flapped against it. She realized it didn't bother her, whereas if ever Darren were so messy, she'd be both embarrassed and annoyed.

"Greg," she continued, anxiety giving an edge to her voice.

Greg looked startled. "Yeah?"

"I'm really sorry if I've made things difficult for you, and for Penny."

"You've done nothing wrong, Ruthie." He leaned back, looking weary. "Neither have I, for that matter. A misjudgement maybe, but I don't think I could have foreseen it."

There was a long pause as Greg tapped his fingers without any rhythm on the arm of his chair, and gazed ceilingwards.

Eventually he lowered his head. "The trouble is, Penny is chronically short of self-confidence. You might not think it, but she always has been. I've known her all my life – we grew up in the same village, Teignford, where Shar still lives. We kicked around together quite a lot, not as a couple, just part of the village kids. Sam was another one – Phil's cousin. Then Penny left the village to join a dance company, but was often coming back for visits, and we continued to, you know, kick around together. Then when I got back from my visit to the States, I found Sam had got engaged to Tom, and Penny was panicking that we'd all pair off and she'd be left on the shelf." He sighed, grasped the back of his neck and shook his head. "Believe it or not, about a week later she proposed to me."

"She to you? Wow."

"As good as. Jokingly, I thought, but no, it turned out she was serious."

So this, Ruth thought, was why there had been no hint of it during his brief stateside stay. Penny hadn't then been a girlfriend or fiancée waiting for him at home; she'd just been – what? One of the gang.

"You said yes?"

"Not straight away. But she brought it up a couple more times, then she was about to go off on tour and I suppose I thought yeah! Don't miss out! She's something special! We got on well together, we appreciated each other's artistic ambitions, my painting, her dancing and…" He made an awkward movement with his shoulders. "I didn't want to be left behind either. A couple more of the group were also getting it together. So I said yeah, let's give it a go. I think we had a joint or two going at the time! But, and this is the whole point," he looked straight at Ruth and spread his hands in a gesture of 'well-that's-how-it-is', "though we were making a really good go of it, genuine love developing and all that, she was still chronically short of self-confidence, which reached a new low after the accident, and it hasn't recovered much since."

"I'm really sorry." Ruth realized she had tears in her eyes. "Poor Penny. Poor you."

"Unfortunately," more neck grasping, "it can come out as massive jealousy. She's accused me before now of having an affair with Shar."

"Which you haven't?"

"Too bloody true I haven't. I like her in small doses, but she can't half talk."

"Now Penny is jealous of me?"

"Clearly. It doesn't help that we – you and me – get on so well."

Ruth nodded. Despite the awkwardness of the situation, despite the sympathy she felt, she couldn't prevent – she didn't want to prevent – a warm glow suffusing her mind and body at his comment.

"I suppose I could start calling you names in her presence, and bitching about you behind your back?"

He threw back his head, giving an abrupt laugh. "I get your thinking, but I don't think it would work!"

"Perhaps I should just leave?"

"Don't be daft, Ruthie. You're going on Monday anyway, and I invited you to stay, and I want you to stay. It's a terrific tonic for me, having you here. Madam will have to put up with it for another, what," he looked at his watch, "thirty-six hours. Having said that, I reckon I should go up now, otherwise she'll think we're…um, I won't spell out what she'll think we're up to."

As Ruth went up to her bedroom, it spelt itself out in her mind, and continued to do so as she sat in bed trying to dip further into Penny's music hall book.

X

The next morning, Sunday, a Steps Bridge outing was agreed on by Greg, Ruth, and a delighted Frankie. He had already put on his green Young Forester sweat shirt and a pair of khaki cargo shorts, pockets bulging with binoculars, a small camera, a multi-bladed penknife, a compact first aid kit and other equipment without which, it seemed to Ruth, the young explorer would be in great danger from the many hazards to be faced on a trek along the Amazon, rather than a riverside walk in Devon. She expressed wonder and astonishment at every fresh revelation.

Penny, Greg said, would not be joining them as she wanted to phone her sister. It didn't sound to Ruth that he had tried hard to change her mind. Frankie, pockets clanking and rattling, ran upstairs to ask his mother to give his love to Aunty Shar.

Relieved at Penny's decision, Ruth felt guilty at feeling relieved, then annoyed with herself for feeling guilty, and finally settled on accepting that it was all right to feel relieved but not overjoyed.

The journey out to Steps Bridge took them along a winding country road with old-fashioned signposts at two or three junctions, past fields and woods, and past a farm with a notice fixed to its gate offering cheap cider. "Lethal stuff," Greg remarked. They passed a turn-off to the village of Teignford. "That's where I used to live," from Greg; "It's where Aunty Shar and Uncle Jimmy live," from Frankie. On past a large sign announcing they were entering Dartmoor National Park, then another Teignford turn-off, shortly before passing a plain old brick chapel with a wayside pulpit poster warning any passing Dartmoor reveller that THE DAY OF THE LORD IS AT HAND – "Hallelujah!" Greg proclaimed in a deep vibrato. Eventually, they arrived at a row of cars parked erratically on the roadside at the approach to a narrow, humpbacked stone bridge over a river. Across the bridge, they turned in to a small car park and claimed one of the two remaining spaces.

An ancient, bulging, dingy green rucksack on his back, straps dangling and flapping about, some terminating in little rectangles of tarnished metal, others simply frayed, Greg led the way back over the bridge and through a gap in the stone wall and on to a riverside path. To their left, the river, foaming white as it tumbled through boulders near the bridge, grew more placid further upstream. A carpet of yellow flowers covered the far bank and, as they walked on, the woodland to their right was freckled in yellow. Ruth felt intensely happy.

"Daffodil time," said Greg. "It's always a great sight."

"It's so good!" She already had her camera ready and took several photos.

Frankie, who had been holding Ruth's hand, now released it and ran on ahead, then crouched down to examine something before taking out his camera and photographing whatever it was. He was writing something in his notebook when they reached him.

"Look, Ruth, Daddy." He pointed to some fungi sprouting from a decaying tree stump. "I don't know what that is."

"Me neither," Greg agreed, also crouching.

Beside him, Ruth peered at the sprinkling of grey spots, which looked like adolescent acne on the rotting wood. "You'll have to look it up when we get back."

"In his element," Greg said, standing up.

"I must take some photos. Get a bit of a record. Frankie!"

He looked up, grinning at her. She took three photos, two including Greg, before they resumed wandering along the riverbank. Various chirps and tweets and other bird calls accompanied them. A sudden commotion broke out high up in an old oak before a crow came flapping out. The river's ceaseless sibilance was punctuated by loud splashes as dogs plunged into the current after thrown sticks, while other dogs remained bank-bound, watching and barking at their more adventurous fellow canines. Ruth and Greg paused to watch one retriever repeatedly charge into the water, scrabble about on the riverbed, then return to the bank, each time with a sizable stone in her jaws. She dropped each stone on a little mud beach in no obvious pattern before plunging back.

This kind of leisurely outing, she reflected as they resumed their stroll, did not appeal to Darren. He always wanted to do active things: running up steep inclines or using convenient branches and hefty logs as gymnasium equipment to tone up his muscles. He always had to *achieve* something, rather than simply enjoy it. Whereas Greg was happy sauntering along, appreciating the immediate present. It struck her that he no longer loped along as she vividly recalled him doing on the Walden Pond outing. Penny had been right: he had put on a little weight. Not that it didn't suit him.

"Did you come here a lot when you were growing up?" She tried to imagine a Greg as young as Frankie.

"A fair bit, but mainly we liked to go out on the moor itself."

"Who's *we*?" A tiny dart of jealousy pricked her.

"Me and my sisters, and then with Phil and Sam and the others. Out to Wistman's Wood, or on to Hay Tor and the old quarry, or Widdicombe or Princeton and…" As he continued with the roll call of unfamiliar and, to her, exotic place names, she repeated them to herself as though each were a charm or a spell. He referred to birds she had never heard of – meadow pipits and stonechats, wheatear and the Dartford warbler. "Ravens, sometimes," he continued. "Skylarks if you were really lucky, but usually a case of hearing them way up high, but invisible." As he told her of hours spent swimming in the rivers, sketching, picnicking, the occasional night sleeping wild, she could hear a wistfulness in his voice.

Occasionally signs warning of riverbank erosion directed them away into a daffodil- and celandine-strewn swathe bordering the woodland, until the path brought them through patches of wild garlic back to the river. Where the river was untroubled by dogs, the surface of the water, with its little vortices and eddies, glittered in the sunlight like crinkled kitchen foil. A woodpecker was hard at work somewhere nearby.

The riverside path was beaten earth, uneven and crisscrossed by tree roots, many just breaking the surface, making a pattern like that of a miniaturized choppy sea. Other roots had brief sections clear of the earth, trip hazards to catch the foot. Which was what happened. After they had been walking some while, Ruth's foot caught in a loop of tough root. She stumbled and Greg grabbed her arm, and she swung in a clumsy arc, feeling, even as she nearly fell, a tiny electric thrill as the back of one of his hands momentarily brushed against her breasts. She held on to his arm as he heaved her up, an action which brought their faces close together. A strong urge to kiss him welled up, but the next moment his face had drawn away from hers. The urge died down, replaced by a slight panic. *For pity's sake! He's married, you stupid idiot.*

"Are you okay?" he was asking. "Is your foot okay?"

"I think so." She had pulled her foot free of the root and tentatively put some weight on it. Only the slightest of twinges, but she couldn't stop herself exaggerating a limp as she tried walking.

"Hey, come on." Greg adjusted his hold so one arm was fully around her waist. "Let's get to that bench."

Continuing to hop, enjoying the sensation of Greg supporting her, she made it to the bench and sat down. Only then did he release his hold. Taking off his rucksack and swinging it onto the ground, he sat beside her as Frankie came bounding up.

"Why are you sitting down?" he demanded.

"Ruth may have twisted her ankle." Greg tugged at the rucksack zip.

"Does it hurt?" Frankie asked her a little too eagerly. "Is it bleeding?"

"No blood, just a bit of a twist. I got my foot stuck in a root."

"I twisted my ankle once," Frankie said. "I jumped down the stairs and didn't land properly. It really hurt. I had to have it bandaged for weeks and weeks. Can I have a look? See if it's swollen?"

"Probably not a good idea," Greg said before she could answer. "Just let Ruth rest it. I know," he pulled a metallic vacuum flask from the rucksack, "We'll stay here for a bit and have our coffee. There's a Coke in here somewhere for you, Mr Attenborough, if you want to dig it out."

"Roger! I mean, neat!" Claiming his drink, Frankie dashed off again to investigate a heap of old logs and branches.

"Bugs and fungi." Greg laughed.

She drank a little of the coffee from the plastic beaker, then started to blow on it as though it were too hot, disguising the fact that she was trying to calm herself down. It still troubled her that she could contemplate kissing him, even though she had neither willed it nor carried it out.

"It's lovely here." She gazed at the river, which had taken on a continuously changing piebald aspect, but now the sky clouded over and the river colour changed again to a near uniform dark grey.

"Damn!" Greg said.

"Language, as Frankie would say! But why damn?"

Greg pulled out of his rucksack a battered-looking sketch pad. "Voila!" He waved it at her, a quizzical, almost triumphant look on his face.

"You're going to do some sketching?"

"You excel yourself, my dear Watson, with your powers of deduction. Some sketching indeed, only the light's disappeared."

"It'll come back," she prophesied. A sense of déjà vu had struck – she could see herself on a previous occasion, thirteen years ago on the other side of the Atlantic, sitting among other trees, close to another stretch of water. "What are you going to sketch?"

"You."

"Me?" She leaped up. He had completed the déjà vu for her.

"Hey! Hey!" He grabbed her arm in alarm. "Mind your ankle."

"Ow," she said, a fraction late, allowing him to support her as she sat down again.

"Are you okay?"

"I'll live." She gave the ankle an unnecessary rub. "But I'm so excited you want to start sketching again."

"See what influence you have over me." He produced his pouch of clips, pencils and erasers from the rucksack. "What you've been saying to me about getting back to doing my art—"

"Nagging?" She looked at him archly.

"Okay, nagging. But very nice nagging! What you've been saying, and what I told you about Lucy, really brings it home that I mustn't let myself use her death as an excuse for not trying. Especially as I reckon she had a pretty good eye. She liked drawing. Yeah, I must at the very least get back in the saddle again, and if the horse won't budge, I'll have to…er, I don't know where this metaphor's going!"

"You're going to give it a go? I think that's wonderful, and *of course* you can sketch me as the first of the new phase! I'm flattered. This is so exciting!"

"What I'm thinking is – ah, hip-hip-hooray, the sun's come out again! It looks a pretty clear sky now." He had paused to look up, shading his eyes in a way that made him look like an intrepid explorer gazing on an unknown land. Stout Cortez. "What I'm going to do," he resumed, turning back to her, "is a sketch of you here, by the river, in the same pose as the Walden ones." His initial hesitancy had given way to enthusiasm. "I'll take some photos to go with it, then I'll be able to work them all up into a full painting to go with the others – complete the sequence, but in Devon, not Walden. How about it? *Neat* or not?"

"Neat!" She laughed. "A *neat* idea!"

"So back on the bench, please, and I'll just…" He heaved a couple of logs from the other side of the path to sit on. Ruth arranged herself on the bench under his direction, a strange sensation to be doing his bidding, far more self-conscious than her twelve-year-old self had been. His energy, his very *aliveness* at doing the ordinary things preparatory to drawing, simply thrilled her. She so hoped this genuinely would be the beginning of a new artistic phase for him – and she was the trigger... It was hard not to break out into an idiotic grin.

Greg arranged his pencils in a container on the ground and fixed metal clips to hold the sketch pad, although the intermittent breeze still caught and lifted the corners of the cartridge paper. He sat on one of the logs with his legs stretched out in a way that reminded her of how he had once sat in Aunt Lou's house.

A further item from the rucksack was a broad-brimmed canvas hat, of the sort she expected to see corks dangling from. "A present from Oz," he confirmed, minutely adjusting it on his head. "Shar bought it for me when she and Jimmy were out there on hols and it'll be my artist's hat from now on. What do you reckon?"

"Very becoming."

"Becoming what, though? That is the question. Now." He held up a pencil. His face, though in half-shadow from the hat, looked slightly flushed. "Let us begin. Head to the left a bit, please. No, sorry, my left, your right. That's it. Focus on, I don't know, a tree branch. That's it." He paused for a few seconds as though meditating, then began.

The old sound, familiar from years back, of his pencil moving over the sketch pad seemed to set up a vibration inside her, like a violin string being played causing a companion string to resonate.

As he sketched, two dogs came to investigate before their owner called them away; a family group with three small children paused to watch for a minute or two; an elderly man smoking a cigarette came and stood in Ruth's line of sight until she opened her eyes wider and gave him her best basilisk stare, whereupon he dropped the cigarette, trod on it and shuffled off. Frankie dashed up with news of flowers he'd been identifying, gave Ruth a wave and dashed off again.

Greg worked on. Ruth had entered a state of non-thinking, a suspension of time, until a loud sighing groan broke out, and she glanced round to see him tossing his hat in the air. She could also see beads of sweat on his face, and he was breathing heavily, as though he had run an ultimately taxing race, putting in an extra burst in the closing stages.

"Oh, yes!" His smile was so broad that the usual lop-sidedness was smoothed away. "This is going to be so *good*!" He leaned the sketch pad against his log seat at an angle, and although Ruth craned her neck, she could only see the sketch edge-on. She made to get off the bench. "Stay there a minute more." He held up his camera. "Just a few piccies for additional..." He didn't finish the sentence as he fiddled with the controls; then, "Don't say cheese," and the shutter clicked several times as he moved to catch her from different angles.

"Finished? Let me see." She scrambled off the bench feeling absurdly excited. "Can I see?"

Greg picked up the sketch and turned it towards her. She stared in amazement, and shivered. He had captured – or was it *released*? He had *released* – something essential about her: the look he had seen in her eyes, the set of her mouth, the faintest suggestion of her youthful freckles – what was it? Although she was gazing at a depiction of herself, it was nothing like looking in a mirror – no, it was more like looking through the mirror to her soul.

She turned her attention from the sketch to the sketcher. "You said," she uttered the words slowly, deliberately, "that art had deserted you. That you might never pick up a pencil or brush again. You fraud!"

Greg laughed. "Oh, Ruthie, I can't help but be inspired by that face of yours!"

He approached her, put the sketch pad on the bench, thought better of it and slid it into the rucksack, then turned to Ruth and opened his arms. "Come here, you," he said.

They hugged. She felt herself being drawn into a warm, comfortable enclave of existence, safe and desirable, one of unquestioning acceptance.

"Why are you two hugging?"

She broke free and took a step back. "Because your daddy is very clever, Frankie."

"Look." Greg picked up the sketch pad and turned it so Frankie could see. "That's what I've been doing. What do you think?"

As Frankie solemnly studied his father's work, seemingly to ensure that justice had been done, she quickly sneaked several more photographs of father and son.

"Golly." Frankie finally gave his verdict. "It's lovely, Daddy. Are you going to do more drawings now?"

"Not this very instant, but I will, I will. Ruth's really inspired me. Hurrah!" Greg picked up his hat and again threw it into the air. It was a poor throw, which, coupled with a flicker of breeze, sent the hat into the river. Greg and Ruth simultaneously burst out laughing.

"I'll get it! I'll get it, Daddy!" An excited Frankie darted forward to the bank and started to scramble down.

"No, Frankie, come back." Greg made a grab for him and failed as the boy jumped the last foot or so, landing with a squelch at the water's edge. An eddy in the river had jammed the hat against a knot of protruding tree roots, and with the help of a stick, Frankie hooked it up and held it aloft as a trophy. Greg stretched out a hand and hauled Frankie back onto the bank. "Well done! A gold star for a great rescue." He took the sodden hat and clapped it on his head. "What do you think?" He paraded around like a fashion model, water raining down from the hat. His high spirits were infectious. Frankie danced one of his jigs. Ruth cheered and clapped.

"I'm hungry." Greg abruptly stopped parading about. "Let's get something to eat. There's a nice little garden café in Teignford."

They headed back along the river to the car. On the way, Ruth had her right arm through Greg's crooked left, while Frankie held her left hand. She forgot to limp.

xi

Her ocean floor was in trouble, threatening to split, erupt, thrust another island up to extend the archipelago of remembered emotion. This was not what she had expected. Or intended. To find herself falling in love with the same man again – the one now driving her back to his house, to his wife, with their son in the car – was absurd. This visit was meant to have been a few days of amusing reminiscences along with the opportunity to thank Greg in person for the kindness and understanding he had shown her thirteen years earlier, but that had barely, if at all, been mentioned. She had always viewed that episode in retrospect as a schoolgirl crush – surely it *had been* a schoolgirl crush? But as she had sat on the bench by the river and he had been madly sketching away with that fantastic concentration of his, she had longed for him to put down his sketch pad and pencils to take her in his arms. To hold her securely, reassuringly. Was what she was feeling simply a recrudescence of that crush? Or a brand-new phenomenon, in that peculiar way love affairs develop because of the *chemistry* between two people or their *being in tune* with each other, or whatever other fatuous non-explanation one might want to drag up. How much was it fuelled by a longing to comfort him for the way Penny treated him?

On their arrival back in the late afternoon, with her emotions all over the place, she longed to have time to herself while Greg was attentive to Penny; but Frankie begged her to come and look at some of his treasures. He looked so hopeful; how could she refuse?

His bedroom sparked more déjà vu. Although noticeably smaller than her own room at his age, it had the same mix of untidiness punctuated by outcrops of extreme neatness; where she had had books on painting and drawing, his books were on natural history; where she had her sketch pads and pencils, he had a collection of variegated pebbles and tree bark; and on the walls instead of paintings, drawings and a David Cassidy montage, he had colour charts of butterflies and moths, of mushrooms and toadstools, of frogs, toads, newts, and other amphibians.

"Daddy got them for me, from his newspaper. Mummy gave me the money to buy this." He opened a drawer and proudly took out a bulging book. His *Young Naturalist's Book*.

She sat next to him on his unmade bed under the window, which looked out onto the Green, and watched as he slowly turned over the pages, looking up at her at every fresh entry. With her mind's eye she could see her twelve-year-old equivalent, desperate for Greg's approval as he had studied her paintings and drawings. What must he have thought of her then? What did he think of her now? Suppose—

"Ruth, do you like these?"

She wrenched herself back to the present. Frankie was holding open a double page of – of what, exactly? Pond skaters, they were pond skaters, carefully drawn and coloured – legs splayed, little ripple marks spreading out.

"Hey, they're neat! I saw a few this afternoon on the river when your dad was drawing me."

"There'll be loads more soon."

"You did this all by yourself? That's fantastic."

"Daddy did help a bit." Frankie touched the ripple marks. "He showed me how to do those. It shows they're moving."

He turned to another page, startling her with a coloured drawing of a butterfly. A red admiral. There was something odd about it: the wings seemed to be attached at slightly different points on the body, and the white spots on the left wing were definitely larger than those on the right. The drawing had been done on a separate sheet and glued into the book.

"That didn't come out very well," Frankie admitted, peering at it. "I managed to get really close to it and started to draw it, then it flew away. Then a bit later there was another one on a flower, or I suppose it might have been the same one, so I crept up and drew the rest. Almost. But it flew away as well, so I had to finish it by looking at the chart."

"So, it's a composite?"

"No, it's a red admiral."

"Silly me." Despite her still churning emotions, she smiled. "It's really very good indeed…your book. I'm so impressed."

"I'm glad you like it." There was a catch in his voice. He gave a sniff, then wiped his nose with the back of his hand.

"Frankie? What's wrong?"

He sniffed again. "You're going tomorrow, aren't you?" he said mournfully.

"I'm leaving in the morning, yes."

"When will I see you again?" He spoke in a low voice. "You will come again, won't you? Come for longer."

She didn't reply immediately. The intense anguish she had experienced on that final evening of Greg's visit back in 1973 was so sharp in memory. Frankie repeated his sniff. She put an arm around him.

What could she say? Yes, she would love to come again. The thought, the image, of being regularly in Greg's company, of sharing some of his life even if they couldn't have a love affair, was intensely appealing. But there would be so many complications, and right now she had to focus on Frankie. She knew what he was going through. *Be kind, be reassuring.*

"I'd like to, but I honestly can't say exactly when that would be. I've got my work and everything."

"We can't really visit you in America." Frankie banged his heels on the floor, but whether from frustration or resignation, she couldn't tell. "Because of Mummy. She doesn't like travelling. It's painful for her to be in a car or a train, and I suppose an aeroplane would be even worse. I know Daddy wouldn't leave her behind. Nor would I. She can't manage on her own."

"Tell you what." She cuddled him a little more. Shouts were coming from outside. "There's nothing to stop you writing me, is there? I'd love to hear from you. You can keep me up to date with all of this," she tapped his *Young Naturalist's Book,* "and I could send you photos of flowers and trees that you won't have seen. It'd be a bit like visiting the States without moving from here. How about that?"

The shouts from outside were louder. Two voices, perhaps three. They sounded like boys' voices. Head down, Frankie mumbled something.

"What was that?" Ruth asked.

"Will you send some photos of yourself as well?"

"If you like. Of course. I'll ask Darren to take some." She winced. Would the reminder of her boyfriend upset Frankie? The mention of Darren upset *her*! She had written him twice from Italy, and had been disconcerted to realize she simply hadn't known what to put other than touristy-type clichés. "I'll let you know about anything interesting that's going on for me," she offered, "if you like?"

Frankie nodded.

"Is that neat?" she asked encouragingly.

He nodded again. "Neat," he repeated miserably.

Further shouts. Frankie's name could be heard.

"Oh." He turned, knelt on the bed to peer through the window, then waved frantically. Also turning round, Ruth could see two boys standing on the Green, only a few yards away, one waving, the other holding a soccer ball. The front doorbell rang.

"I must go." Frankie scrambled off the bed.

*

Ruth collected her sponge bag and towel, then paused at the door to the bathroom. The front door had slammed shut behind Frankie, and now the indistinct and overlapping voices of Greg and Penny rose from downstairs. She gazed unseeingly at the explosion of colour at the top of the stairs that was the Freedom Dance Collective, but a sudden shrill "No!" from Penny, immediately followed by the sharp click of the sitting room door being closed, put paid to further eavesdropping.

The bathroom was cold, as was the radiator, but when she turned on the thermostat control, the pipes made alarming clanking sounds. She hurriedly turned it off again. The shower unit over the bath seemed to respond as it should, and she stripped off; but by the time she was ready to step under it, the water had turned scaldingly hot. Rotating that control a fraction had no effect. Rotating it more, and a few seconds later the deluge became horribly cold. More tiny adjustments until the temperature was reasonable. At last! She stepped under the shower, tilted her head back and allowed the water to course over her, frustration fading, but her feelings still in turmoil from the afternoon. As they had walked back to the car, Greg's supporting arm round her, Frankie holding her hand, they must have looked like a loving couple out for a walk with their son. If only...

They'd had some lunch in a sweet little tearoom overlooking a garden, its walls festooned by various climbing plants; seen Buttermilk Cottage where Greg had grown up; and gone to call on Greg's sister-in-law Charlotte, who, to Ruth's relief and Frankie's big disappointment, was out.

Replaying all this, she shampooed her hair – but before she could rinse it off, the water was turning cold again, the pressure dropping. A tap downstairs being run? She had noticed this happening on a previous occasion. Still standing in the bath, she adjusted the shower head, but the downward rush of water was creating eddies of cold air. Shampoo was stinging her eyes.

The water pressure returned, and the water temperature increased. Unhooking the shower head, she was able to rinse her hair well enough before the danger of scalding herself returned.

Towel wrapped around her, she sat on the little chair to catch her breath. Why should having a shower be such an endurance test? Fantastic artist though Greg might be, he was clearly useless as far as maintenance tasks were concerned. That, she reflected, was the one area where Darren scored highly. Admittedly he didn't do the hands-on work himself, but whenever her place or his needed something doing, he was onto it, phoning the plumber, the electrician, the handyman. But that was about it – otherwise Darren was, what? Ordinary. An ordinary young American. Kind enough, and helpful enough, but a life partner? No, no. She had been kidding herself that he could be Mr Right. He probably *was* Mr Right for someone else, but no, not for her. Whereas Greg...? *Oh*, why *is he married?* She was sure her feelings for him differed *qualitatively* from any feelings she'd had towards previous boyfriends, all the way from sweetly shy Tom up to cave-dwelling – strictly speaking, cave-exploring – Darren.

As she resumed drying herself, she realized there was another area in which Darren did score highly, and she had no way of comparing Greg. For a moment, she paused in her drying and started to touch herself – only to snatch her hand away almost immediately. *Don't be so stupid!* She hadn't thought of sex once when in Italy, even in the presence of some *gorgeous men*, as she had put in a card to Donna, and, she told herself sternly, she didn't need it right now.

She had forgotten to bring into the bathroom a change of clothes. Wrapped in the towel, she opened the bathroom door to return to her bedroom. More sounds, louder sounds, from downstairs. High-pitched shouts from Penny, a banging sound, more shouts. Though muffled by the door between the hall and the main room, several words were distinguishable. "*That slut!*" suddenly penetrated the door like a power drill, followed by "*weird or something?*" Shocked into immobility, Ruth remained by the stairs, gripping the top of the newel post with one hand and her towel with the other.

Greg's raised voice, not exactly shouting but determined to be heard, followed, his words indistinguishable and then cut short by another Penny yell: "*I'll say what I fucking like! She fucking is!*" Now Greg's response could be heard: "*Will you bloody calm down!*" There was a further scream from Penny followed by a crash. Immediate silence, then Greg's raised voice again, "*Oh for God's sake, now see what you've gone and bloody done,*" with Penny's screamed riposte, "*You shouldn't have fucking ducked!*" at full volume as the door was wrenched open.

Ruth turned for her room but her towel slipped from her grasp. Naked, groping for the towel, half hoping Greg would look up and see her, she watched in fascination the drama below: Greg striding to the front door, fiercely pulling it open, Penny's unmuffled scream of "Why don't you just fuck off forever, and take that fucking slut with you!" and the front door slamming shut behind Greg.

Ruth stumbled to her room and dived beneath the duvet, shivering and trembling with cold and anger. If she were a slut, wouldn't she right now be plotting to get Greg into her bed, not anguishing over how much she couldn't allow herself to be in love with him, even though she was? Should she go downstairs and confront Penny? But what good would that do? Probably make things worse for Greg, without resolving anything. If Penny thought she was a slut, so be it. Greg clearly didn't.

Thank heavens she was leaving tomorrow. She wouldn't go downstairs but stay in bed to keep warm until it was time for the evening meal. How on earth would she – or any of them – survive that?

She became aware of different voices, coming from outside. The sound of boys enjoying a kick around, recalling Brad and his friends doing the same when Greg had visited. Such innocent times...

*

A tap on the door roused her from a fitful doze. "Yes? Come in. No, wait a minute." She grabbed the sweater from the chair back and hurriedly pulled it on, then made sure the duvet covered everything else. "All right!"

Greg entered looking more round-shouldered than ever, as though he were invisibly carrying on his shoulders an old-fashioned milkmaid's yoke with two full buckets. "How are you doing? Had a bit of a kip?"

"Just resting."

"Slight change to meal plans." Greg advanced further into the room. "The menu's had to be re-written, and we're going for traditional English."

"Sounds good! Meaning what?"

"Fish and chips. If that's okay by you. I'm just going to get them."

"I'll come with you."

Greg held up his hand like a traffic cop. "Probably not a good idea. Frankie'll come."

There was a pause. Greg was staring at the floor.

"Anything I can do to help in the meantime?" Ruth asked.

Greg looked up. "No, it's fine, thanks. Um, Ruth? I was wondering – you may have heard something earlier…"

She stiffened. What could she say?

"Penny and I had a bit of a…" he hesitated, "ding-dong."

"Ding-dong?"

"Ding-dong. Disagreement."

She pursed her lips and gave a tiny shake of the head, hoping to convey deep puzzlement. "I did sort of hear something going on when I was in the shower, but I couldn't tell what. Everything was clanking too much."

Greg looked relieved. "I'm afraid Penny's pain has been pretty severe all day…"

So much for Vanessa the healer, thought Ruth.

"…and she gets short-tempered and a bit paranoid, and we end up rowing. I was getting something from the bureau. She comes in, accuses me of snooping, I tell her don't be daft, we row, and she chucks her stick at me. Like a javelin." He mimed an inept javelin thrower. "Luckily, she's a rotten shot, but I'm afraid the Tiffany got hit amidships and went down with all hands."

Ruth gave an involuntary snort of laughter. "Sorry! But the image that conjures up is, well…"

"Straight out of music hall?"

"I guess so!"

They burst into laughter.

"Enough of all this frivolity," Greg said when they stopped laughing, "but sorry if you thought you must be staying in a madhouse."

"That's all right. After all, it's none of my business. Unless you want to off-load some more?"

Greg shook his head. "No need – but thanks for the offer."

She waited a few seconds, then asked in an artificially bright voice, exaggerating her American accent, "What fish are they frying tonight, buddy?"

Greg clapped his hands. "Haddock and cod are the house specials, and I recommend the cod. The chef's signature dish is sausages in batter. Frankie likes that. Want one?"

"Oooh yes! Let's go native!"

"Mushy peas?"

"What are they?"

Greg looked puzzled. "They're peas," he said slowly, as though explaining to a simpleton, "peas that are, er—"

"Mushy?"

"You got it! I'll get a pot. That's three cod, two sausages between us, peas brackets mushy, and three portions of chips. Best in the region!"

"Let me—" She reached for her purse.

"No, no. I'm getting."

Greg left.

Ruth relaxed her face after the strain of the brief burst of faux-jollity. She'd stay upstairs until Greg and Frankie returned.

No way was she going to risk going downstairs to put herself in Penny's firing line.

'*That slut! Weird or something? Why don't you fuck off forever? Fucking slut...*' Would he fuck off forever? What would she do if he did? But then there was Frankie to think of. What would be best for him? She got on well with Frankie, but that was hardly relevant, was it? For all Penny's mood swings, she seemed to have maintained a good relationship with him.

xii

She woke early the next morning to sounds from outside: a barking dog; a voice shouting a farewell; a front door banging shut; the detonation of a car door slamming; a car engine turning over, failing to start, turning over again and finally starting; the car driving away and silence returning. No, not quite silence – she could now hear the faint twittering of birds, punctuated by harsh cries of rooks or crows or similar. Greg and, no doubt, Frankie would know. She went to the window, pulling open the William Morris curtains to gaze across the Green at the silhouetted trees where untidy clumps of nests were still just visible, though half-hidden by the burgeoning spring foliage. Three or four large black birds were circling. A cyclist was laboriously making her way up the slight incline from the other end of the Green, and two small boys were creeping along, snail-like, illustrating something out of Shakespeare's seven ages of man.

She turned from the window, closed the curtains and switched on the light. The previous evening had been fine, though dinner hadn't improved her opinion of English cuisine. What on earth was so special about fish and French fries – only they weren't French fries but some obscenely obese British abomination – saturated in vinegar and salt, and battered – in both senses of the word – sausages? As for mushy peas – Frankie had cheerfully called the mass of green sludge dolloped on the side of the plate *cat sick*, which said it all, though he and Greg had happily tucked into it while it took all her resolve not to gag. But food aside, the evening had been a happy time – no Penny, who remained in her room, Frankie taking her up some food on a tray; laughing at an old episode of *M*A*S*H*; listening to Frankie – sitting next to her – reading aloud the latest entry in his *Young Naturalist's Book*; chatting easily with Greg about what plans the Boston Art Foundation & Gallery had for the rest of the year.

But now – sounds of household doors opening and closing, someone in the bathroom, someone running down the stairs – now her visit was nearly at an end. She'd better get started with packing.

*

She was still packing when there came a knock at the door and Greg called out, "Hi. Are you decent?"

"Come in."

"We're about to have breakfast." He looked in. "Frankie and me. Join us?"

Frankie said so little over breakfast that his Rice Krispies were more communicative. He kept looking at her then quickly lowering his eyes. She didn't try to make conversation with him, but talked with Greg about what her itinerary was, when they should leave for the station after he returned from taking Frankie to school, and how long her flight back would be.

Breakfast over, Frankie responded wordlessly to Greg's "Quick teeth clean!" by clumping upstairs. She hadn't realized before how expressive footsteps could be.

When he came back down, she braced herself for an outpouring of emotion, reproducing her own embarrassing outburst on the last evening of Greg's visit, but Frankie stood stiffly in front of her, neat and tidy in his school uniform, hair brushed, and said in the manner of someone who has been coached, "Bye-bye, Ruth. It's been neat meeting you. I mean, lovely meeting you."

"It was really lovely meeting *you*, Frankie. Very special," and as a whispered addition, "Would you like a hug?"

Frankie glanced at Greg, evidently received the go-ahead, then smiled broadly and gave her an eleven-year-old boy's equivalent of a bear hug. As she responded, she looked at Greg over Frankie's head, and he gave her a thumbs up.

At the front door, when he was in the car, she waved vigorously and he waved back even more vigorously with both hands as the car pulled away. Within seconds, it had turned out of sight round the end of the terrace. She returned to the kitchen for more toast and coffee.

Penny appeared, clad in an exotic, Japanese-style robe. "It's back to the States, then?"

"Yes." Difficult to judge Penny's mood. "Thanks for your hospitality."

"I hope your journey back is straightforward." Penny sat, again partly obscuring Max Miller with his Cheerful Chappieness. "But I'm not going to lie and say I wish you were staying longer."

"Oh!" Ruth couldn't think how to respond. Penny was at least being honest, she supposed, but honest*ly*, what a thing to say.

"What I will tell you," Penny's voice was firm, not its habitual feeble tones, "is that you wouldn't succeed even if you had been here a month."

"What?"

"You're not going to take him away from me."

"*What*?"

"Don't think you can rescue Greg. Greg does not need rescuing."

"I'm not trying to take Greg away from you! Or rescue him!"

"Aren't you? I think you are, but you're not going to succeed."

"What are you talking about? Why would he need rescuing?" Ruth stared across the table at Penny, whose elfin features were curiously passive, in contrast to her voice and her words. Her hair was bundled high on her skull in an auburn sculpture, kept in place with a couple of long, Japanese-style hair sticks with decorative tops. The bobbly white scar on her temple, like an ancient hieroglyph still to be deciphered, weirdly challenging.

Now here's a funny thing! the Cheerful Chappie assured Ruth behind Penny's back.

"He doesn't need rescuing," Penny repeated scornfully. "I'm talking about me and Greg. Greg and me. Us. Greg's a good man. We've been through rough times together and we've stuck by each other. That means everything. You think he needs rescuing from me, don't you? Shar used to think that too, but she was wrong, very wrong, and—"

"This is nonsense, Penny!" Ruth burst out. "Yes, I like Greg, I like Greg a lot, of course I do, otherwise I wouldn't have wanted to visit, would I? But I wasn't coming to take him away from you…or rescue him or anything like that. Where did you get these ideas from?"

She held Penny's gaze, stiffening in alarm as Penny reached up and slowly pulled out first one hair stick and then the other from her coiffure. For a fraction of a second the sculpture stayed put, then it came tumbling down as an auburn avalanche, obscuring the scar once more and coming to rest draped over both shoulders. Still Penny clutched the hair sticks, her hands, bunched into fists, resting upright on the table, the sticks vertical, pointed ends uppermost, like spikes cemented along tops of walls to deter intruders.

Ruth turned her eyes to the door. It was open, but to reach it she'd have to go past Penny. *Keep calm. Just keep calm.*

"He told me about you." Penny, maintaining her gaze, spoke in a low tone. "When he came back from that visit. We'd just started dating. He said you were a great kid. Full of you, he was. How old were you? Ten?" Her features lost their passivity, now distorting into a grimace as she uttered the numeral. Still the hair sticks remained vertical.

"Twelve. I was twelve." Greg had thought her a *great kid*? Despite the situation, a starburst of happiness irradiated her heart, like a firework lighting up the night sky.

"Twelve? That's worse. Old enough to know better!"

"Know better? Know better about what?"

"Oh, come on. Trainee vamp, and you're still at it. Trying to seduce him."

"I was a kid!" The starburst abruptly blotted out. "I had a crush on him! I wasn't seducing him then, and I'm not trying to seduce him now! Don't be absurd. Didn't you ever have a crush on anyone?"

Penny seemed to notice for the first time the hair sticks in her hands. With an unvoiced 'Oh!' she let go of both and they fell onto the table, one then rolling off and dropping to the floor. She looked at Ruth with a ghost of a smile. "Did they worry you?"

"They did a bit!"

For a moment it felt that they would both laugh, but the moment passed and Penny's face resumed its passivity. No laughter, but at least the tension in the kitchen had moderated, the emotional temperature lowered. Thankfully Penny hadn't kept pressing her about her feelings for Greg. Would she have been truthful if she'd had to answer? Probably not, but she would have hated herself for denying her feelings, however inconvenient they were.

"What did you just ask me?" Penny swept back her hair but it tumbled forward again.

"I said, didn't you ever have a crush on anyone? As a kid?"

Penny nodded slowly. "Oh yes."

"Well, then."

"Only it was a long-term crush. Lifelong. On Greg." A tear trickled down a cheek before her head drooped. She muttered something inaudible.

Ruth leaned forward, asking, "What?" softly.

Penny looked back up, tossing back her hair again, again exposing the scar. "Greg!" she said fiercely. "I fell in love with Greg long, long before we ever got married." Her statement sounded like a defiant confession. "It started as a crush, but it became a lot more as I grew up. We lived in the same village; did you know that?"

Ruth nodded.

"Oh, he told you *that*." Scornful Penny hinted at re-emerging, but reasonable Penny resumed. "I always wanted him to fall in love with me, ever since I was knee-high to a…whatever it is. But he never seemed interested, beyond being a good friend and one of the village gang. I adored him all through our teenage years. The pains of unrequited love. I know them, you know." She had become mournful, and was twisting a lock of her hair, then pulling it and wincing.

Ruth nodded, thinking, *Don't we all?*

"I started to joke with him about how much time we were spending together, but it wasn't a joke to me. I was absolutely over the moon when he said he'd marry me, after I'd made all the running, and finally," her voice rose in incredulity as she repeated, "he said he would marry me. So we did, pretty well straight away. Two days' honeymoon, then I went on tour, would you believe. He was great about it." She pointed at the cafetière. "Pour me some of that, will you?"

"It's not one of your herb things."

"I want coffee."

Ruth collected a mug with *Starry Night* on it from the cupboard, wishing she could give her Munch's *Scream*, and tipped in the remains from the cafetière.

Penny took it, drank some, and resumed. "We got married and it was fine to start with. All hunky-dory. Frankie had *come along*, as they say, Greg was painting away, and running his art classes, they were really popular, and in due course I was able to get back to dancing, working with the Collective, then – oh shit, has he told you about Lucy?"

Ruth nodded again. Her own eyes were filling with tears, knowing what was coming.

Penny shook her head despairingly. "What an utter darling she was! Hard work, of course, all kids are. Have you got children?"

"No."

"You don't know what you're missing. Utterly besotted with her, we both were. With Frankie as well. Then, shit…it all got destroyed." Her shoulders slumped and she started to sob. Ruth hesitated, then reached across the table and gripped Penny's arm. Penny grabbed Ruth's wrist and clung on, sobbing even more.

"I'm so sorry" was all Ruth could think of to say.

"That fucking accident." Sobs continued, punctuating what Penny said. "Losing a child is seriously the worst thing ever. I know it was my fault too, the accident. I'm amazed I didn't get done for dangerous driving – I suppose they thought I'd been punished enough. A terrible, terrible time. Ever since then, I've been terrified…"

"What of?"

Penny glared at her, removing her grasp on Ruth's arm. "Terrified Greg will leave me. Don't you see? Don't you get it?" Scornful Penny making a take-over bid.

"He's not going to do that, is he?"

"No? Look at me. I'm a fucking wreck. I'm amazed he's stuck with me so long. That's the trouble with Greg. He's too nice." The sobs had subsided. "He's a good man. But even a good man will have his breaking point, and I know I keep pushing him, like I *want* him to leave because I deserve to be punished. Accusing him of being rubbish, of the accident being his fault."

"Why?"

"Why what?"

"Why are you…" she hesitated, "so nasty to him? And say those sorts of things?"

Penny fiddled with the remaining hair stick. "I suppose I want to hurt him," she muttered, not looking at Ruth. "I know it's stupid, but I can't stop myself."

"But why on earth would you want to hurt him?"

Penny shrugged a shoulder. "Why do people self-harm? Because I know that's what I'm doing. Self-harming. I'm terrified he actually *will* leave because of it. Because of me. I *hated* it when Greg said he'd had a letter from you, asking to visit. I was terrified. Then you turn up, and it's worse than I feared. You're young and pretty, and you're arty, and you get on really well with him, and I'm overcome with jealousy. *Intense* jealousy, like acid. It happens. I know I behave like a shit, but…" Her voice tailed off.

Unable to stem her own tears, Ruth could say nothing as Penny resumed sobbing, but took Penny's hand and sat in silence.

xiii

At eleven o'clock, Ruth was sitting at a small round table in the station café, hemmed in by her large suitcase to the right and the bulging backpack to the left, once again checking her tickets and documents. All in order – as they had been when she had last checked. The station was busy, noisy with amplified announcements, multiple conversations from nearby tables, hisses and clankings from a coffee machine, and the racket of trains pulling into and leaving the many platforms. On the table were copies of a magazine on current British culture, featuring an article on Goldsmiths College, and of *Private Eye*, both recommended and paid for by Greg. She still felt confused and saddened by the final encounter with Penny, with her mix of hostility, honesty and pain. Should she have made a greater effort earlier on to engage with Penny? But how could she have done that? Anyway, she had gone to *visit* Greg, to catch up with him in just a couple of days. She was not there to *steal* him. All the same, she was aware of a slightly uncomfortable feeling verging on, but not quite tipping into, guilt.

Still some time to go before her train was due. It seemed that Greg, now at the counter buying coffee, had deliberately set off for the station far earlier than necessary, claiming that the traffic could be unpredictable. Which perhaps was so, but there had been no roadworks or slow-moving convoys or diversions, and it felt far more likely that he had wanted to make sure there would be time for them to have a final coffee and chat together. Or maybe because it allowed him to get away from Penny for a while? Or both? In her current state of mind, she was pleased to take the final-coffee-and-a-chat as the main, if not the sole, reason.

She had already decided not to give Greg any details of her and Penny's conversation, giving a very brief, anodyne version preceded by an airy "Oh, we were fine," to which Greg had responded with a grunt that may or may not have signified doubt.

He reappeared with a tray of cappuccinos, croissants, and paper serviettes sporting the *Great Western Railway* logo. He sat down. "Well, Ruthie," picking up two sachets of sugar, "it's been lovely to see you these last few days, and I'm sorry you're going so soon, but, erm…" He busied himself tipping sugar into his coffee.

"But perhaps it's just as well I'm not staying longer?"

"Maybe." He stirred his coffee slowly as if it were a meditative practice. "I'm really sorry about how Penny's been. I didn't think she'd be quite so difficult and negative. I saw your visit as an opportunity for something *normal* – for us both – a guest staying, getting out a bit, letting us focus on something other than illness." He sighed and dropped the spoon noisily onto the table. "Having you here for a few days has been great for me—"

"And me!" How lovely to hear him say that. "I really have enjoyed seeing you again and spending time with you."

"Well, thanks. But there's more." He stroked his beard. It looked neatly trimmed, and, moreover, he was wearing a smart – or smartish, or smartish for him at any rate – not crumpled, that is to say – sports jacket and grey flannel trousers. Nothing ostentatious, but he definitely looked spruce. Why the sartorial upgrade? Was he hoping or intending that she would notice? Which she had. Was he in turn, she suddenly wondered, taking in how *she* looked as they prepared to say goodbye for however long?

The ambient noise made conversation difficult. She leaned towards Greg to hear him better, and he responded in like fashion. To others, she thought, they could have been two lovers having a final intimate conversation before a long separation.

"That sketch I did of you yesterday," he resumed, beard stroking concluded, "at Steps Bridge. I just know it's going to make a terrific painting! I can see it up here already." He tapped his head. "It'll be one of my best ever. No doubt about it. What you've done, young Ruthie," he reached out and squeezed her hand, "is, you've fired up the old imagination."

Ruth felt her mouth drop open. "Have I?"

"For far too long, I've been in the doldrums."

He retained his hold on her hand. And was it her imagination, or a trick of the café lights, or had the blueness of his eyes become really brighter and sparkling? With hope?

"Okay, granted," more hand squeezing, "there's been a shedload of shit to contend with over the past few years – all to do with the accident. I've been guilty of adding to the shit by, er, practically giving up on art, and resenting the situation."

"Hardly *guilty*."

"Well, responsible if not guilty. But if it weren't for Frankie, you know – having to be there for him, and wanting to be there – who knows? I could have gone completely under. Then there's Lucy." He breathed out heavily as though contending with physical pain.

"Yes."

"I mustn't allow her death to put an end to my painting, must I?" He held her gaze. The emotional tension emanating from him was like a form of radioactivity. If she were a Geiger counter, she was sure she'd be exploding with clicks. "It'd be like blaming her. That'd be intolerable. I have to switch from feeling: *Lucy died so I've given up on art*; to: *Lucy died and my art will be dedicated to her*. I want her to be proud of me – or rather, I want to be able to believe, to know for sure, absolutely certainly, that she'd be proud of her old man and his art if she were alive to see it." He slumped as though saying that was like putting down an immense burden.

"Of *course* she'd be proud of you! Of course she would. Greg! Listen to me! She'd be as proud of you as anything, and if you go on – I mean, *when* you go on to create even better art, who wouldn't want to be the inspiration for that?" She stopped. Was she conveying another message? That she too was an inspiration, a catalyst of Greg's renaissance? Of course she was. "Like me," she said, "nagging you!"

"Um, encouraging me! But yeah, you have brought this about – not just because you nag...*encouraged* me, but mainly because you're *you*. The Steps Bridge painting will be the first in the new, er, new *whatsit* of my art."

"Epoch?"

"The very word, epoch of my art." He gave his coffee a quick swirl and drank some. When he put the cup down, he had acquired a foam moustache on top of the original.

"What about Penny?" She picked up a paper serviette. "What's she going to think of another picture of me? You'd show her, I assume? She's not exactly my number one fan, is she? Won't she object?" She made to wipe away the foam moustache, but Greg let go of her hand and took the serviette to do it himself.

"Frankly, my dear, I don't *give* a damn." His Clark Gable was execrable. "I have to paint what I have to paint, whatever she might think. But what *will* please her is that she's right: I need to cut down on the booze. Lose a bit of weight. I have been knocking it back a bit as, well, you know, a bit of a reaction to everything that's happened. Getting back to doing what I really ought to be doing will make a difference with that as well. But what do *you* think?"

She put her unclaimed hand on her chest – it felt as though Greg's words had injected her with a highly potent recreational drug. Everything was buzzing, magical, hallucinatory. "Yes, yes! That would be so good if you really got back into it. And surely Penny would be pleased? Surely!" The final encounter with Penny came flapping up into consciousness again, and her earlier resolve not to talk about it now seemed pointless, even wrong. "I need to tell you something. About her."

"Sounds ominous."

"Hmm, it's just…when you were taking Frankie to school, we did have a bit of a chat…rather more than I said earlier."

"She didn't have a go at you, did she? I'm so sorry, but—"

"No, no, listen. It started that way, yes, but then she actually started to cry. She was saying how terrified she is that you'll leave her."

"What?" Greg stared at her, then blinked rapidly several times, as though trying to clear his vision. "Why would she think that?"

"She's afraid that how she behaves, things she says like the accident was your fault, might make it happen. You leaving her, I mean. But she can't stop herself. At least, I think that's what she was saying."

Greg grasped her other hand, and she fleetingly wondered if they looked like lovers enacting a scene from *Brief Encounter*. When she fell silent, Greg leaned back, eyes closed, still holding her hands.

"Silly bitch," he said softly.

Shocked, it was her turn to stare. "What?"

"Silly bitch. As Tom would say."

"Who? What? Tom who?"

"Tom. Tom Good. You remember." He leaned forward, releasing one hand to tug at his beard. "The comedy we watched. He called Barbara a silly bitch because she was doubting or wondering if he loved her. Of course he did!"

"Irony," she remembered. "I do get it."

"I don't know how many times I've tried to make it clear to her we're in this together." Greg spoke over her. He looked forlorn. "Even if it weren't for Frankie, I wouldn't leave her. The trouble is, she feels reassured for a day or two, then something gets into her head and it all kicks off again. I lose it from time to time, yeah, which doesn't help..."

"I got into her head, I suppose. Before I even arrived."

"Don't go blaming yourself, Ruthie."

"I don't."

"Good. But when I get back, a spot of extra attentiveness is called for."

"With a bunch of flowers?"

To her surprise, Greg gave a shout of laughter before asking, "Ever had a dozen cellophane-wrapped red roses chucked at you? Thorns to the fore? Bloody painful!"

"I guess."

"Not recommended. That was early on. I can't remember what I'd done wrong on that occasion; criticized Margot Fonteyn or something, I imagine. Since then, my ducking reflex has become fine-tuned, otherwise that lamp would still be with us. All the same, I'll think of something unchuckable." He looked at his watch. "Hey, Ruthie, I'm afraid you should get going. You have to get over the bridge, platform five."

"Oh. Sure."

They stood, looked at each other quizzically, then wordlessly embraced. When they broke apart, she hoped he wouldn't notice tears forming.

"Got your ticket ready?" Greg picked up her backpack and went with her to the barrier. "Sorry, I'm not allowed through without a ticket."

"So, it's goodbye here?"

"Yeah, 'fraid so."

Another embrace.

She allowed him to help get the backpack on, then extended the handle of her suitcase. "It's been so good seeing you again. Now, you must get on with everything you have to do for the open studio. Sock it to 'em!"

"Yes, ma'am." He gave an American-style salute.

"Give my love to Frankie."

"Yeah. You give my love to Lou and Harold, will you? And your mum. Keep in touch, Ruthie. Let me know how the gallery's going."

On the other side of the ticket barrier, she turned to wave. Greg raised his hand, but when she next turned, he was making for the exit and the car park, hands thrust into his jacket pockets. She watched until he was out of sight, on his way back to Penny.

*

The hours on train and plane passed uneventfully, at least externally. Though not yet a seasoned traveller, she was not one to experience undue fears or anxieties other than a concern for the security of her passport, tickets and luggage. There were no cancellations, no particularly annoying fellow passengers, no worrying announcements; queues all moved forward at reasonable speeds; officials were courteous, efficient.

On the plane, she read the article on Goldsmiths and its prestigious array of artistic alumni past and present, and dipped into *Private Eye* but found many of the articles and cartoons too parochial, so took out a trashy paperback she'd bought at the airport. She read it in between dozing, eating a plastic meal and, mainly, thinking. Scenes from the previous days replaying before her mind's eye, both pleasurable – the welcoming hug from Greg, their day together in Exeter, sitting by the river as he sketched her, Frankie's devotion – and the less pleasant – that awkward first meal, Penny's scream of *that fucking slut*, and the one and only conversation with Penny. And thinking about Greg, her feelings for him, and what might have happened but didn't... *A crush*, she told herself repeatedly, *is a crush, is a crush, whatever your age.* And crushes get you nowhere. But she continued to wallow – knowing she was wallowing, wanting to be wallowing, insisting on wallowing – in the pleasure of the pain of nothing developing between them.

Silly bitch, she admonished herself. A real, unironic, silly bitch for allowing herself to indulge in romantic fantasy. Maybe Greg had some tender feelings for her, but not of a wife-leaving nature or intensity. It was unambiguously clear that a combination of love, loyalty, and total commitment to Frankie kept him where he was. At least she hadn't made a complete fool of herself by declaring undying love in an adult equivalent of her adolescent eruption, and expecting him to reciprocate. She turned hot with embarrassment at the thought that she might have done, and for a while she stopped wallowing, only to resume it after a few more pages of novel trash.

One thing had become clear, though… Darren. Such a relief! No more avoiding the obvious that marrying Darren was a no-no. A no-no of stupendous proportions. The realization, as though she hadn't known it all along, that her feelings for him were really no stronger than liking. Except, admittedly, in bed, where sexual desire temporarily drove away all other considerations.

What *had* she been thinking of in allowing, for even a fraction of a second, let alone the months of wavering about it, their sexual compatibility to drive forward the possibility of actually marrying him? For someone else, he may well turn out to be the ideal all-round husband, not just in bed, but that someone was not her. Never could be her. All so clear now.

How would he react to being told that his generous gift – as he would surely see it – in offering to marry her was being returned to sender? Softly, she began to sing the Elvis number, then broke off abruptly, saying, "Oh, sorry!" to the passenger beside her, who smiled wanly. She'd have to consult the expert on how to handle it – Donna, with her experience of ending relationships. They'd laugh about it, no doubt – but she'd keep to herself the counterbalancing strength of her feelings for Greg.

*

In this manner her thoughts revolved for some hours, along with further bouts of dozing, eating and trashy reading. Until a change in the noise of the engines, followed by an announcement from the captain, told her that she was once again under stateside skies. The plane started its long descent back to her everyday life.

Also by R N F Skinner from SilverWood

The first novella about Ruth:

These Years: 1973

When Greg, a professional artist, visits American relatives, he triggers a crush in 12-year-old Ruth. An aspiring artist herself, she dreams he will be so impressed by her talent that he will fall in love with her, but happiness at being in his company is clouded by knowing he is about to return to England. She may never see him again. School friends both tease and encourage Ruth, but her family, except for a sympathetic aunt, are oblivious to the joy and anguish of young love. These few momentous days in Ruth's life rush to a denouement in the last hours of Greg's visit.

A touching account of one girl starting her journey into adolescence.

What they say:

"[To] someone who has been that 12-year-old girl with an unrealistic crush, Ruth is a believable and sensitive depiction of adolescent emotion… a heartwarming and compassionate portrayal of a familiar family dynamic, infused with humour and care."
Ella Woszczyk (Exeter Today)

"Deft, elegant, and exquisitely articulate…. With a sharp eye for the telling detail and excellent sketching in of secondary characters."
Prof T.A. Unwin

"A vivid picture of [a young girl's] feelings at the stage of early adolescence …The emotional highs and lows … are treated with touching poignancy and gentle humour."
Clinical Psychologist Prof. Harry Procter

"Don't be fooled by the length of this book. It is a powerful read… Certainly took me back to my youth and evoked the era well. A master story writer."
'Pat' on Amazon

ISBN 978-1-80042-275-9   RRP £9.99

Still Crazy…

When Phil, an undergraduate at Cambridge University, performs in cabaret at a party, he meets and falls in love with Melanie. As she in turn appears to have fallen in love with him, he cannot understand why she then plays hard to get, even after he learns of the traumatic events that shaped her teenage years. But the influence of former boyfriend Simon is still strong, and she and Phil part. Twenty-five years later, both now married, they meet again by chance and resume their relationship. Soon each faces a tough choice: will Melanie decide on love or loyalty? Will Phil commit to his estranged wife or return to his first love?

"This is a wonderful novel, beautifully written, that threads its way through the lives and loves of its characters who step vividly out of the pages. A delight to read." The Rt Hon Lord Smith of Finsbury

ISBN 978-1-78132-991-7   RRP £11.99

After All…

A collection of short stories and scripts, including *The Lure of the Footlights* featuring Phil, the male protagonist of Still Crazy…, before he meets Melanie. The scripts constitute a small selection of comedy sketches written and performed over many years, including 'Evans', the sketch with which the author gained membership of the Cambridge Footlights; 'Dead Safe', introducing the Health and Safety Officer of the Afterlife; 'Encountering Ourselves' with a dodgy group therapist; and the 'Steeplechase for Saints and Theologians' where St Paul and Thomas Aquinas compete with others to win a Crown of Glory.

"Great writing … [this] collection of stories and sketches is both profound and hilarious… I heartily recommend it."

Dr Gordon R Clarke, author of 'Someone Else's Gods' (SilverWood 2022)

ISBN 978-1-80042-202-5   RRP £10.99